OPERATION AFRIKA

In the summer of 1942 the hard-pressed British 8th Army were desperate for a victory in the Western Desert, but Field-Marshal Rommel, the Commander of the Afrika Korps, had yet another ace up his sleeve. He had not reckoned with one-eyed Lieutenant Crooke, V.C., the ruthless C.O. of The D troyers. Crooke's Destroyers were the onl ones standing between Rommel and fir l victory in Egypt. Under Crooke's ʰ ership they set off on one of the war's t bizarre missions, to find the Red Oasis the missing Chief-of-Staff of the ptian Army.

OPERATION AFRIKA

OPERATION AFRIKA

by

Charles Whiting

Dales Large Print Books
Long Preston, North Yorkshire,
BD23 4ND, England.

British Library Cataloguing in Publication Data.

Whiting, Charles
   Operation Afrika.

   A catalogue record of this book is
   available from the British Library

   ISBN   1-84262-283-8 pbk

First published in Great Britain in 1975 by
Seeling Service & Co.

Published in Large Print 2004 by arrangement with
Eskdale Publishing

Dales Large Print is an imprint of Library Magna Books Ltd.

Printed and bound in Great Britain by
T.J. (International) Ltd., Cornwall, PL28 8RW

THE DESTROYERS: OPERATION AFRIKA

'If you are murderers, as they say you are, let me have more of you.'
Prime Minister Winston Churchill to Mallory's Destroyers, Chequers, November 1942

SPECIAL UNIT 'M-D' (MALLORY'S DESTROYERS)

Crooke, Mark. B. 1911. Education, Repton and Sandhurst. Gazetted 2nd Lt. Essex Rgt. 1933. Third Division, Palestine 1936. Attached GHQ, Cairo, 1938. Joined his regiment, Western Desert, 1939. Volunteered for Long Range Desert Group, 1940. Capt. Promoted Lt. Col. 1941 and awarded M.C. Participant Rommel Raid, 1941. Victoria Cross and invalided to U.K. Promoted Col. 1942. Court-martialled and demoted to 2nd Lt. July 1942. Returned Egypt.

Jones, Alamo, Lone Star. B. 1900. American. Education, Public School 40, Dallas, Texas. Member of Texan National Guard. Pancho Villa Expedition, Mexico, 1916. Western Front 1917–18. *Croix de Guerre.* Variously employed Texan oilfields. Unemployed 1929–33. Volunteered Abraham Lincoln Battl. International Brigade. Service Spanish

Civil War 1936–39. Polish Army 1939. Transferred French Foreign Legion 1940. Deserted. Joined British Army 1940. Sentenced to death for murder, 1942, reduced to 9 years, Egypt. Joined 'Special Unit M-D', August 1942.

Stevens, Stephen. B. 1912. Education, Tottenham Court Rd. R.C. Elementary Schl. Borstal. Various employed 1930–39, hawker and barrow-boy. Volunteered for Army 1939. 28 days' detention, B.E.F. 1940. Court-martialled and sentenced to 10 years' imprisonment. Joined 'Special Unit M-D', August 1942.

Thaelmann, Ernst. B. 1910. German. Education, *Altona Volksschule. Max Planck Gymnasium,* Hamburg. Full-time official of *KPD* (German Communist Party), 1929–33. Arrested 1933 and imprisoned Dachau Concentration Camp. Escaped 1934. Went underground, Germany, until 1935. Emigrated. Various jobs. Joined Foreign Legion 1939, transferred British Army 1940. Suspected of high treason. Sentenced to indefinite imprisonment 1942. Joined 'Special Unit M-D' 1942.

Kitchener, Ali Hassan Muhammed. B. unknown. Education, unknown. Variously employed. Guide, brothel tout, purveyor of pornographic photographs, Port Said. Joined British Army 1939, transferred to Grenadier Guards 1940. Wounded three times, Western Desert. Court-martialled for theft and sexual assault. Sentenced to five years' imprisonment 1942. Joined 'Special Unit M-D' in the same year.

Peters, Albert. B. 1917. Education, Durham Street Council School. Joined Coldstream Guards 1931. Posted India 1931–34. Palestine 1936. France 1940. Posted Western Desert 1940. Promoted CSM. Awarded Distinguished Conduct Medal and Military Medal (with bar). Arrested for cowardice under fire 1942 and sentenced to five years' imprisonment. Joined 'Special Unit M-D' in August 1942.

ONE: THE MISSION

'If the Germans pull it off, it means they'll capture the Suez Canal and there'll be nothing to stop them until they reach India … it could mean the end of the British Empire.' *Admiral Godfrey, Director of Naval Intelligence to Commander Mallory, August 1942*

1

The heat was intense and the sun struck like a sharp knife across the eyes, but the three men, crouched almost naked in the white sand, did not notice the heat or the glare. They stared in silence across the sparkling blue of the Mediterranean. The plane was obviously going to land.

'It's one of ours, Sarge,' said the driver from Barnsley confidentially.

'Famous last words,' the skinny corporal commented pessimistically.

But the sergeant sprawled out full length on the hot sand did not hear them; his whole attention was concentrated on the seaplane which was now touching down.

Behind them, in the shelter of the cove, the rest of the men from the 53rd Transport Company, XXX Corps, were getting dressed. They were noisily enjoying the first day off most of them had had in a year of driving their lumbering Bedford lorries 'up the blue', as the Eighth Army called the Libyan Desert.

The sergeant shielded his eyes and tried to make out the seaplane's identification signs. As he moved his arm, the brown flesh of his back rolled up along the line of scars left by a machine-gun at Dunkirk two years before. They looked like buttonholes cut by a pair of rusty shears.

'Get the bren!' he snapped.

'But it's fixed to the cab of the three-tonner, Sarge,' the skinny corporal protested.

'Get it.' He did not look round at them. He had made up his mind.

The corporal nodded to the driver. 'All right, you heard, didn't you? *Get it!* And tell that shower down there to stop making that ruddy noise!'

The driver dropped his rough white towel. Naked, he pelted down the sandhill to the trucks.

The seaplane had made a clumsy touch-down and was taxiing closer to the shore. The sergeant screwed up his eyes against the dazzle. He knew his planes. Since that terrible moment at Dunkirk when the Me had singled him out from the rest of the thousands crouching helplessly on the sands, he had learned to recognize every enemy plane. It had become a passion with him, and now he knew that he was looking at an old pre-war Heinkel 59 seaplane.

Then he saw the black cross against the brilliant white of the metal fuselage. But what the hell was an enemy plane doing a hundred miles behind British lines? Admittedly this was a lonely stretch of the coast – the Eighth Army's main coastal road was a couple of miles off – but still, 'I wonder what dirty work they're up to,' he asked himself.

He had no time to answer his own questions. The young driver came panting back, his face wet with sweat, kicking up sand around the two NCOs.

'Here's the bren, Sarge,' he said, 'and I brought the two spare mags.'

The sergeant grabbed the gun and slapped the magazine to check that it was securely fixed. He tucked the butt into his shoulder and pressed his chin down on it. Swiftly he went through the movements of the trained infantryman he had been before the German fighter had got him at Dunkirk and he had been downgraded to the Service Corps.

The seaplane was definitely coming to a stop. The foam at its floats had vanished. The prop was revolving even slower. He could make out the radio aerial now and the dark blur of the pilot's head behind the perspex of the cockpit.

Another man had aimed at the fuselage. But the sergeant's mind was full of the beach at Dunkirk, the horrible stench of blood and mutilated flesh, the flames and smoke, the Me roaring down, the purple crackle along its wings as its eight machine-guns poured lead at him, the vicious stabs of pain and then oblivion. Now at last he was at the other end of the machine-gun. He aimed at the dark blob of the pilot's face.

The range was 200 yards. 'Now!' he shouted and squeezed the trigger. The bren kicked at his shoulder. The sergeant swung the gun from left to right to spread its fire. The perspex of the cockpit shattered. The dark blob of the pilot's head disappeared abruptly.

'You got him, Sarge!' the driver cried exuberantly.

Momentarily he relaxed his finger on the trigger. The seaplane was still moving, but erratically, as if suddenly blinded. He pulled the butt hard into his shoulder again and pressed the trigger. There was no answering kick.

'Christ!' he cursed. He'd already fired a whole magazine in his excitement. 'Bloody fool!' he cried, more at himself than anyone else. 'Hey, give me the other mag.'

The corporal dropped into the sand, snapped off the magazine and fitted the new one. The seaplane had straightened up in the meantime. Obviously someone had pulled the pilot from the controls and taken over. Its prop started to whirl again. Twin crests of foam appeared at its floats. Desperately the man leaning over the pilot's shattered body was trying to take off, heading for the open sea. The sergeant knew it was a matter of seconds before the German made good his escape. He pulled at the bolt handle. It wouldn't move. 'Christ on a crutch!' he roared.

With the calloused palm of his hand he struck the bren a tremendous blow, pulled at the bolt which now slid back. Swiftly he snugged the butt into his shoulder. The Heinkel was hovering a few feet over the waves. Some two hundred yards to the south there was a sandhill. Once behind that the plane would be safe.

He took careful aim, trying to control his breathing. Then he squeezed the trigger. The butt kicked back. The air was full of the acrid cordite smoke. The red tracer – every third round – stitched the blue air like a stream of angry hornets. The aim was dead on. He caught the plane in its single radial

19

motor. Bits of gleaming metal started to fly from the cowling.

'It's on fire,' the corporal shouted excitedly. 'Look at that!'

Thick oily smoke, licked by violet flames, streamed from the fuselage. The seaplane came down hard on the waves. But it kept its course. In front of it the sandhill loomed up. Fifty yards – thirty – twenty. The sergeant took his finger off the trigger. The plane roared forward at a hundred miles an hour, flames and smoke pouring from it, then vanished from sight. A moment later there was a tremendous crash. A pillar of thick black smoke shot into the sky. Then there was silence.

The front of the seaplane had folded up like a banana skin under the impact. Standing there the awed RASC men stared at the wreck, with the oil dripping onto the sand. 'Look at the poor bastard,' one of the drivers said. 'Looks as if somebody had thrown a handful of plum jam at his face.'

The sergeant followed the direction of the finger pointing at the dead pilot. He was still holding the bren, as if he needed it to stay upright while he surveyed the results of his handiwork. 'Have they all had it then?' he asked tonelessly.

The skinny corporal, who had waded into the water to check for survivors, shouted from the rear of the wrecked Heinkel: 'Ay, they're all goners, Sarge. I thought–'

But he never finished his sentence.

'They're not, yer know, Sarge.' It was the young driver shouting from the top of the sandhill behind which he had run to be sick when they had rounded the cove and first seen the bloody mess inside the crashed seaplane. 'Come up here and have a look at this.'

A bunch of them raced up the hill to where the driver stood looking down at something in the sand. The sergeant caught up with them and pushed his way through the circle which had formed around the driver. 'What is it?' he demanded roughly.

The driver did not answer. Instead he nodded at the sand. A line of wet footprints was visible, with a strange little dark blob of liquid between each step. The sergeant bent down and touched one of the blobs with his forefinger. Slowly he held up his finger for them all to see. It was stained a pinkish-red.

'Blood,' he said.

2

Commander Miles Mallory was bored. On this particular August morning even Room 39, the heart of British Naval Intelligence did nothing to excite him. In spite of the constant comings and goings of pert-bottomed little Wrens bearing another batch of top secret reports from all over the world to the desk-bound Old Etonians who, like himself, had transferred from the City to the 'Wavy Navy' in 1939 everything seemed routine, stale and boring. The usual reports about the harbour facilities at Kiel's *Kriegsmarinehafen* or the appearance of a new minefield off Norway on the Hull–Murmansk convoy route left him cold.

He leaned against the fireplace and stared through the window at the Horse Guards Parade with a barrage balloon tethered above it in the rain. The war and Naval Intelligence were, at this particular moment, a bore. He needed action – violent action – or a new woman.

But the Commander was not fated to

spend that night with one of those elegant society women he preferred. For at that moment the buzzer sounded and the green light above Admiral Godfrey's door flashed, indicating that he wanted his chief assistant.

The Director of Naval Intelligence beamed at him as he entered. 'Good morning, Miles.'

'Good morning.'

As always Mallory omitted the 'sir'. Godfrey was not offended. He had got used to Mallory's idiosyncrasies by now. As he had once told another admiral in the United Services Club, half in admiration, half in anger: 'Why the feller had the audacity to tell me to my face that there are only two persons you should address as sir – the King and God!' But in the two years that the Admiral and his chief assistant had been together, he had never regretted the fact that he had taken Mallory into Naval Intelligence. The man had proved his worth on a dozen or more highly confidential and sometimes dangerous missions and by 1942 Mallory was the only man to whom he told all his secrets. Now once again the Admiral had need of the ex-merchant banker's daring, unconventional thinking and flair for getting things done.

Indicating a chair, he handed him a glossy

photo. 'Take a look at that Miles.'

Mallory obeyed and handed it back. 'A bit ghastly, isn't it?'

The Admiral nodded, admiring once again the younger man's apparent lack of curiosity or shock. In thirty years in the Navy, most of them in cruisers, he had met a lot of tough men proud of their inability to be shocked, but never one like Mallory.

'The photo was taken last week about a hundred miles behind our lines between Alex and a little place called Alamein. For some reason that plane – a Heinkel 59 seaplane – tried to land there. One of our units spotted it and some bloody fool Army chap shot it up and literally wiped out all the crew.'

'Typical of the pongos,' Mallory remarked.

Godfrey chuckled in admiration. Even now the other man evinced no curiosity about the horrible photo of the mangled contents of the German naval plane. 'I said all the crew. But that was not quite accurate. One of them got away. The Army chaps tried to trace him. But as usual they missed the boat. He circled round them and before they'd tumbled to it, he'd stolen one of their trucks and let down the tyres of the remaining ones. Field Security found the stolen vehicle a day later, abandoned on the outskirts of Alex, with this in the cab.'

He reached inside the red leather-topped desk, which had once belonged to 'Blinker' Hall, the famous (some would have said 'infamous') head of World War One Naval Intelligence, who had brought the United States into the war in 1917 almost single-handed. He pulled out a soiled white uniform jacket and smoothed it out on the top of the desk.

Mallory's face lost its reserved look. 'German naval officer's uniform,' he said.

Godfrey nodded. 'Yes, *Kapitänleutnant*.'

Mallory picked it up and turned it over. There was a bloodstained tear in the back. 'The pongos winged him, I see.'

'Yes; not badly. The army could never shoot, but he bled all right. Field Security found a couple of towels which he used to staunch the flow. They found them when they discovered he'd changed into their kit.'

'You mean–?'

'Yes, the beggar had the audacity to sort out the gear they'd left in the lorry when they went bathing. He fitted himself up with one of their blouses and an odd pair of shorts. Nondescript stuff, as far as I can gather, you know those types in the desert.

25

They dress on the careless side. Suede shoes and civvies trousers and all that sort of nonsense. At all events he kitted himself out well enough to get past the redcaps.'

'He must have been in a hurry, though,' Mallory said, running his hands through the pockets of the tunic. 'He left this.' He drew out a crumpled photo.

Admiral Godfrey smiled. 'Yes, I know. We pulled the same trick on the PM yesterday.'

'The PM?'

Godfrey was pleased. He had broken through his assistant's reserve.

'Yes, we – that is Joint Intelligence – showed it to him yesterday at Number Ten.'

Mallory picked up the photo once again and studied it.

Despite the water stains and faint brown circles, which might have been blood, it was quite clearly a typical pre-war German snapshot, on yellowish paper with the characteristic crinkly continental edges. It showed a group of young officers in *Wehrmacht* uniform posed against a high brick wall, beside the typical red and white pole of the entrance to an official building. Holding it close to his eyes he could just make out the legend on the pole's red and white sign: *Hoechstgeschwindigkeit 15 Km.* 'A barracks,' he murmured, thinking aloud.

'That's right, Miles. A barracks outside Berlin.'

'You know that much then?' he queried.

'Yes, the brown jobs are not that bad at their business. Occasionally they come up with something. We gave them the photo on Wednesday for identification. It took them twenty-six hours, but they made it – a barracks on the outskirts of the German capital.'

Mallory replaced the photo on the table. He had regained his reserve.

'But of what interest is this to us, Admiral?' he asked politely but coldly.

'Little at the moment, save for one thing. That barracks houses the Brandenburgers, the sabotage troops of our old friend Admiral Canaris.* And what is a naval officer off the coast of Egypt doing with a picture in his pocket of a group of young soldiers who belong to German Intelligence's élite spy and sabotage battalion?'

Mallory nodded. 'Undoubtedly,' he said carefully, 'you have some idea on the subject, Admiral. Perhaps you have been able to tie the thing together?'

*Admiral Canaris was head of the wartime German Intelligence Service, *die Abwehr.*

27

Godfrey chuckled. 'As they say in the language of the *Herrenvolk*, Miles, you are able to hear the grass growing.' He cleared his throat. 'Well, the scenario for this particular plot by our friend Canaris *might* go like this. Nouri Pasha, chief-of-staff of the Egyptian Army, is not exactly a friend of this country. Nouri Pasha, you will remember, was born in Salonika while it was still part of the Turkish Empire. He's a Doenmes – old Jewish family converted to Islam. And ever since he was released from British internment in Malta in 1920 – he'd served with Ataturk – and came to Egypt to join its Army, he has been a thorn in the side of the administration in Cairo. Sir Miles Lampson frankly hates his guts.'

Mallory's forehead creased in a frown. 'Wasn't there something with his son, who disappeared with the 1937 Youngblood expedition into the desert?'

'Yes, Colonel Youngblood was in the Coldstreams. He disappeared with the boy, who was a fervent nationalist. He belonged to that group of young officers around Nasser and Sadat whom we're watching now. Afterwards Nouri Pasha always maintained that Youngblood was responsible for his son's death. No one knows of course because the leaders of the expedition disappeared and all the authorities could go on were the wild tales of the bearers and servants who they had left behind at the last base. At all events thereafter Nouri got really anti-British and anti-Farouk, filling the junior ranks of the Army with young Egyptians of like sympathies. In 1941 we learned from a delicate but sure source that he had betrayed the defensive plans of our Egyptian frontier positions to the Germans.'

Mallory smiled at the old fashioned euphemism for cipher breaking, but he did not interrupt his chief's exposé.

'At the time we let the matter go. We were doing fairly well in the desert. But now things are different. You know yourself how desperate the situation is out there. Four weeks ago a very smart pilot officer attached to the Egyptian Air Force managed to prevent an unauthorized flight leaving his field for an unauthorized destination. He did it without causing a diplomatic incident and he'll get a gong for it. However, that's not the point. The point is the plane's passenger. It was El Nouri Pasha!'

'And it's pretty obvious what his destination was?'

'Yes, Rommel's headquarters. Naturally

the PM didn't waste time. He told Lampson to see Farouk and tell him what his chief-of-staff had been up to. And, for a change, the King acted. He put Nouri Pasha under house arrest in his place just south of Cairo. And that's the situation at present. But the question is whether he's going to stay there. Everybody knows we're on our last legs in the Western Desert. It's an open secret in Whitehall and the War Office that Rommel is poised on the Egyptian border ready for his last attack. And although our chaps out-number his, the Eighth Army is demoralized and browned off with the whole show. And as for the new commander, Montgomery, he's an unknown quantity.'

'Who?'

'Some new chap that the PM and Alan-brooke have dug up. He's already on his way out to the Eighth. Brooke apparently had him as one of his div commanders in France in forty. He's supposed to be quite good, but a bit of a prig.'

Mallory absorbed the information in silence and waited for his Chief to go on.

'Well, as I was saying, this will be Rommel's last go. Hitler can't support him any more, what with the burden of the fighting in Russia, etc. So what will Rommel do? He'll go for the Eighth with everything he's got. And at the same time he'll try to add weight to his lack of numbers by creating trouble to our rear.'

'You mean Nouri Pasha?'

'Probably. If he could get Nouri Pasha to call out a holy war à la Grand Mufti behind our backs in Egypt, most of the Gippo Army would come out against us, making a hell of a mess of our lines of comunication and rear echelon.'

'So,' Mallory took over, 'either Canaris or his man at Rommel's HQ has dreamed up some new scheme for getting Nouri Pasha out after the failure of the plane attempt and the Brandenburger, whose uniform the pongos found, is the contact man.'

'Yes, and if the Germans pull it off, it means they'll capture the Suez Canal and there'll be nothing to stop them until they reach India. In short, it could mean the end of the British Empire.'

The two men lapsed into silence. On the wall behind them an ancient clock ticked away the minutes. In spite of his outer calm, Mallory's mind was racing. *'The end of the British Empire!'* He knew the Admiral; he wasn't a man given to exaggeration. Of course he was right. After Egypt, India would inevitably go, with the Japs pressing in from one side and the Jerries from the other. Empire manpower was stretched to the limit as it was. There would be nothing to stop the Desert Fox.

'But where do we fit in, Admiral?' he asked, suddenly.

'The PM has given me the job. After all we are the senior intelligence service and the seaplane did belong to the *Kriegsmarine*. So I want you to go out to have a look at the situation in Cairo. You'll find our little friend of the *Regiment Brandenburg* and naturally ensure that El Nouri Pasha does not do a bunk.'

Miles smiled for the first time since he had entered the room.

'Nothing I'd like better than that on a rainy day in London, but I hardly think I'm quite the chap for the job. I haven't been to Cairo since '35 and even then I didn't see much of the place. I was with the delightful young woman you–'

'Enough, Miles. Spare me another of those disgraceful stories of yours. I've already made provision for that particular problem. I'm attaching an expert to you who knows the whole Middle East situation like the back of his hand. He's been out there almost continuously since '35 when he went with Wingate to Palestine.'

'Who is it?'

'Crooke VC.'

Mallory's face dropped. His vision of warm sun, of nubile girls at the Kit-Kat Club and of everything that went with it vanished abruptly. He had heard about Crooke, a fanatical ex-infantry officer cast in the harsh, unyielding Wingate mould who had lost an eye and won the VC on his last mission – an attempt to murder Rommel.

'Colonel Richard Crooke VC,' he said gloomily.

'Second-Lieutenant Richard Crooke,' Godfrey corrected him with a smile. 'Since two weeks ago when he hit the Deputy Commander Home Forces on the end of his rather prominent nose for refusing to have him posted back to the Middle East.'

'Christ! They could hang somebody for that!'

'They almost did. That's why he's now going to be your subordinate!'

'Well, bloody hell,' was the other man's only comment.

Admiral Godfrey smiled. It was the first time in months that he had been able to ruffle the composure of his chief assistant.

'All right, Miles, get back to your flat now and pack what you need. You'll be leaving Croydon in exactly' – he glanced at the ancient wall clock – 'three hours and twenty minutes. The PM has placed his personal Fortress at the disposal of yourself and your subordinate.'

Mallory's answer was a sad, self-pitying groan.

3

'Okay, gentlemen,' the American pilot said, swaying down the narrow gangway of the Fortress, with a portable oxygen bottle in his hand, 'you can go off the booze now. We're coming down below ten thousand feet.'

Mallory did not need to be told twice. Gratefully, he unhooked the sweaty mask and ran his hand across his jaw. He had forgotten to have a shave when they had landed at Gibraltar for refuelling as the American major had warned him he should. Now he was suffering from what the latter called 'stubble trouble'.

The plane started to come down. He

could feel the metal behind his back grow warmer as the temperature rose in the four-engined bomber which had been given to Mr Churchill with its crew by President Roosevelt.

He yawned and looked around the plane. It was a confusing yet orderly mess of fifty-inch machine guns, hung with great gleaming belts of cartridges, oxygen bottles, controls, throttles, mixture levers, propeller plant handles – and a hundred and one other items which Mallory could not identify.

Crooke, squatting in the makeshift canvas and tubular metal seat next to him, had no time for the interior of the plane. His good eye was fixed on the ground below as they swung in from the Mediterranean and crossed the khaki-coloured coast. 'They call it the devil's country, the Arabs do,' he said suddenly. He pointed through the perspex port. 'Down there, only a few miles from the coastal strip, the temperature will be running around 120 degrees in the shade – if there is any.'

He turned and stared at Mallory with the one gleaming blue eye. 'In the thirties before Bagnold started to go into it, the staff wallahs at Cairo used to say that only the bedouin and crazy men could live out there.' He paused and tugged at the black patch that covered the empty socket of the eye he had lost in the Rommel raid the year before. 'Now there are men down there – scores of them, German, Italian, Free French, British – all fighting a private little war of their own.'

Mallory followed the direction of his gaze. They were well within British lines now and the American pilot was coming down even more. At three thousand feet all that Mallory could see was what he summed up to himself as 'miles and miles of bloody nothing'. 'It certainly doesn't look very hospitable,' he said. 'Not exactly a place one could warm to, eh?'

Crooke ignored the pun. His thin, almost emaciated, face was as grim as ever – Mallory had not seen anything vaguely approaching a smile on it since they had first met in Room 39 twenty-four hours before. Inwardly he groaned, but as he had to work with the man on a vital mission, he repressed his feelings and said: 'The place certainly lacks physical features. Isn't navigating a hellish problem down there?'

Crooke seized the bait. Obviously the desert and everything to do with it fascinated him, as it did so many regular British officers who had served in the Middle East prior to the war. 'Yes, but Bagnold was able to pioneer the sun compass before the war. With that, a map and the speedometer of your vehicle you can make out. Admittedly it's dicey, but the only way to find your way is to orientate yourself on any object which sticks out of the sand – a pile of stones, a camel skeleton, even a rusty old bully beef can.' He pointed downwards. 'From here to a place called El Alamein you have an area, bounded by the sea through which vehicles can move. Beyond that is the desert and the Qattara Depression. It covers several thousand miles, its floor four hundred feet below sea level, most of it being made up of salty marsh. The Depression is virtually impassable. So there are only two ways to move east or west – through the coastal plain north of El Alamein or through the devil's country.'

He paused and licked his lips. Mallory watched him carefully. He realized that Crooke was not only ruthless, as everyone in London had told him, he was also a fanatic.

'There are not many men who are prepared to enter the devil's country. But there are a few of us who have always been fascinated by it.' He hesitated, as if he were about to reveal something about himself which he felt he shouldn't. 'Apart from the war itself, down there is the last challenge.' Then he stopped, leaving his last remark unexplained, and without another glance at his companion, turned his head to the port and stared out in silence.

Mallory relaxed in his seat. The temperature was rising rapidly now and he felt the sweat break out on his body with unpleasant warm dampness. Out of the corner of his eye he watched Crooke curiously – definitely one of the strangest men he had ever met. Back at Room 39 he had done a hasty check of the man's records and what little he had been able to find out, added to what Admiral Godfrey had told him, made it clear that Crooke had the potential to become a great soldier – or a great villain.

In '36, as a young subaltern, he had gone out to Palestine with Wingate. For a while he had worked happily with that strange bearded soldier who was now deep in the Burmese jungle behind the Jap lines with his Chindits. But a year later he had broken with Wingate when the latter involved himself too deeply in his support of the Jewish underground organisation, the *Haganah,* which was fighting a guerrilla action against the Arabs. 'He has some sort of bee in his bonnet about the Empire – that the only way for us to survive is to play one rival nationalistic group off against the other and stamp out those which seem to be getting too powerful,' Admiral Godfrey had explained when Mallory asked him.

'After the break with Wingate, he went his own way for a while,' the DNI had continued. 'Then about '38 he started to take extensive leaves, penetrating deep into the desert with the pioneer of that sort of thing, Major Bagnold of the Royal Engineers. By the time the war started he and Bagnold were the most knowledgeable figures in the Service on the Sinai and the Egyptian sand seas. Naturally a man like that treads on a lot of toes. There were those who said he had a brilliant career ahead of him and others who maintained that he'd remain a captain for the rest of his time in the Army. And then there was the business of his wife. After he was transferred from Palestine to Cairo he was always in the desert, leaves, weekend, any free time he had – and she was left to herself. She was pretty, lively and liked parties – and there were plenty of those in Cairo in 1939, with handsome wealthy men only too glad to take advantage of the absence of her husband. Just as the business was becoming public scandal in Cairo, two things happened – the war broke out and Crooke joined his regiment in the Western Desert. One week later his wife took off for Europe with one of her numerous wealthy Egyptian admirers. Nothing has been heard of her since.

'In '40 when Bagnold suggested the Long Range Desert Groups for sabotage work behind the Italian lines in Libya, Crooke was naturally one of the first to volunteer. It was right up his street – free from traditional discipline with a handful of picked fighting men anything up to five hundred miles behind the enemy front. Soon he became famous – perhaps notorious might be a better word – for his ruthless drive, boldness and spectacular if costly missions. Sometimes he and his group would disappear for weeks on end, finally returning when everyone at GHQ had given them up for dead, emaciated, burned black and bearded like the pard, to report an airfield destroyed, a rearline unit panicked or a vital road link broken.

'In spite of the intense dislike he inspired in many regular officers, there was no denying him promotion. In early '41 he was made a lieutenant-colonel, at thirty, one of the youngest in the desert; and naturally when Cairo started to select people for the great raid on Rommel's HQ, it was inevitable that they would pick him to guide the commandos.

'It was a mess from the very start. Intelligence got the wrong house. Rommel wasn't in it. Instead it was full of very wide-awake Germans, with unfortunate results for our chaps. The survivors made their way back to where they expected the destroyer to pick them up. It didn't turn up on time, and the survivors had to scatter.

'Crooke's group consisted of six very tough and experienced commandos when he set off. Eight weeks later when he finally reached our lines, he was alone, mumbling a confused story of being attacked by the Senussi Arabs who had murdered his men. Who knows what really happened? But Crooke survived, minus one eye, his face burned black and his nose shrunk almost to nothing by the sun and his boots worn completely away.

'Of course, the *Daily Express* got on to the story like a shot. They brought him back to the UK still in a coma. Churchill praised him personally in the House. January 1942 was a bad month if you remember and the

PM was glad of any piece of bravery – whatever its dubious background – on the part of a British soldier. A week later he was awarded the Victoria Cross and promoted to full colonel, the youngest in the Army.'

'Yes, I remember all the fuss and feathers,' Mallory said. 'But it was one hell of a performance to make his way back like that with one eye shot away.'

'Oh, there's no doubt about it that the man is tremendously brave,' Godfrey agreed. 'Well, to cut a long story short, everyone in Whitehall thought Crooke would stay in the UK, probably in some staff job. But the chairborne warriors in the War House didn't know their Crooke. With his wound scarcely healed he descended upon them with a request for an immediate posting to the Long Range Desert Group. Naturally they gave him the usual run-around, passing him from office to office until finally he managed to slip into the office of the Deputy Commander, Home Forces. At first the General tried to humour him. When that didn't work, he pulled rank and authority. He didn't understand Crooke's mentality, not one little bit. The latter reacted with his usual direct violence. When the General refused point-blank to send him back to the Desert,

Crooke let him have it right on the nose.'

Godfrey paused and grinned to himself, as if he were mentally enjoying the picture of the somewhat pompous figure of the Deputy Commander, Home Forces, reacting to the first punch on the nose he had probably had since he left his prep school. 'Of course, there was a tremendous stink. Alanbrooke personally recommended to Churchill that Crooke be court-martialled in spite of his rank and decoration. But the PM had somehow taken Crooke to his heart. You know how he likes picking up these strange military characters. So in the end they compromised. Crooke was demoted to second-lieutenant and, according to people close to the PM, Brookie told him: "I want that man out of the country for the duration of the war." And privately he told his cronies at the United Services Club that Crooke would never be promoted again till hell froze over – or at least as long as he was CIGS. So,' he had concluded his thumbnail sketch of Mallory's neighbour in the plane, 'you've got a very, very tough individual on your hands. A man who knows he has nothing to lose – nothing to lose whatsoever. His career in the British Army is finished. Brookie will see to that, believe you me.'

Mallory had believed him. Crooke was on the way out, but if he knew it he did not show it. He seemed transfixed by the dreary brown expanse of the desert below, as if he were returning to some great love.

An hour later the second pilot, a boy who concealed his boyishness with a great swirling RAF-type moustache which made him look like the US Army Air Corps version of Pilot Officer Prune, announced, 'We'll be landing at Cairo in about thirty minutes' time, gentlemen.' He shoved his crushed-up brown cap even further to the back of his head so that it seemed to hang there by sheer willpower and said: 'The skipper says that Heliopolis Tower thinks...'

He never finished the sentence. Instead there was the frightening clatter of cannonfire. Cold air and metal fragments blasted into the plane's interior. The boy's mouth opened foolishly under the silly moustache. His eyes bulged with pain. Then he sank to his knees, blood seeping out of the holes in his coveralls.

Crooke reacted first. He sprang up, grabbing the mortally wounded young officer before he hit the metal deck.

44

'What the hell's going on?' Mallory cried in alarm.

A quick glance through the port answered the question. Two fighter planes, flying abreast, were coming straight at the Fortress. Suddenly violent lights flashed from their orange noses. Then, when they seemed about to crash head on into the bomber, they skidded to the left and Mallory saw a quick flash of yellow, brown and black desert camouflage and twin black and white crosses. 'They're Jerries!' he shouted.

Crooke took this statement of the obvious calmly. Gently he lowered the young pilot to the deck. Carefully he wiped the blood from his hands and opened the man's collar.

Meanwhile the pilot took evasive action. To their rear the two gum-chewing sergeant-gunners who had been sleeping on the mailsacks seized the 50 calibre machine guns at the open ports and began firing. The noise was terrific. Gleaming metal cartridge cases tumbled on the deck in their hundreds. Acrid smoke filled the interior, as orange tracer arched its way towards the two Messerschmitts. But the firing did not put the Germans off. Again they came roaring in at 400 mph. Mallory, pressing his nose to the perspex, saw both planes lurch. For a moment he thought they had been hit, but he was mistaken. Two long cylinders sailed down from below their wings. The enemy planes sped forward at an extra 30 mph. They had jettisoned their extra fuel tanks.

Suddenly a great burst of cold air flew in. Mallory looked up just in time to see a shining rectangle of silver sail past. It was the main exit door. They had been hit.

Now all was nervous, yet somehow controlled, confusion. On the bloodied floor Crooke worked desperately to stem the pilot's wounds. 'Revs', the flight engineer, rushed back and forth draped with great gleaming belts of ammo, trying to keep up with the gunners who were sweating heavily now. The pilot threw the great plane about, trying to evade the Germans, it shuddered under the strain. The fighters were coming in for the kill.

Mallory yelled a warning to Crooke who dropped the pilot's head on the deck. 'He's dead,' he cried above the roar, and pressed himself down close to the body.

This time the attackers' approach was different. While one of them roared upwards, obviously preparing to dive at them from out of the sun, the other started to do some nice deflection shooting from about 500 yards away, dragging up its nose and lowering its flaps to keep the Fort in its sights longer by thus lowering its speed.

A line of holes suddenly appeared along the length of the metal above Mallory's head, as if they had been stitched by some gigantic sewing machine. He ducked. Behind him there was a scream of pain. One of the gunners clutched his shoulder, staggered back from the open port and slumped down on the littered deck. 'The bastard's got me,' he cried, blood beginning to seep through his tightly clenched fingers. Mallory ran to him. He forced the man's hand away from his leather flying jacket. Blood spurted out and covered his breast. The bullet had severed an artery. Swiftly he pulled off the man's jacket. Next moment he ripped off his own tie and set about making a tourniquet.

Crooke, for his part, had seized the gun and cocked it again. By now the pilot had brought the plane down to about five hundred feet. Below them the Fort's shadow raced ahead across the desert. The sun was behind them. Swiftly Crooke calculated that the other Messerschmitt, still hidden from sight, would come in from the port side and from above, with the sun blinding the pilot and rear gunner.

He clenched his hands on the twin handles, swung his gun round and waited. If he had guessed right, the German pilot would rush them and then break off just before he had to face the twin machine guns of the fourth gunner located above the cockpit. For a split second he might be able to get the German's naked belly in his sights.

Suddenly the plane doing the deflection shooting dropped from sight. Obviously the pilot was leaving the way clear for his wingman. Behind him on the other side of the gangway the sergeant-gunner, standing with his fur-booted legs astride, started to pound away. To their rear the tail gunner joined in. The noise was earsplitting. But both of them were blinded by the sun's glare. Crooke counted three. Then the German was there. The blue belly of the Me, not more than a hundred and fifty yards away. The gun pounded in Crooke's hands. A stream of tracer hissed towards the fighter. Then, with a great roar, the Messerschmitt exploded. A black lump came hurtling towards the Fortress. It was the body of a man, his knees tucked into his stomach, revolving like a diver doing a somersault. It came so close that the one-eyed soldier could see the piece of white paper flapping from the pocket of the black leather jacket. Just before it vanished from sight, it was followed by a small round object revolving frantically as it raced after the body. It was the pilot's head!

The death of his fellow pilot frightened the second Me away. With one last angry burst of his cannon, he broke off and roared away to the west. In a matter of seconds he was a small black speck on the horizon. A minute later he was gone altogether.

The gum-chewing gunner, who had managed to keep his wad in his cheek throughout the action, dropped his gun, staggered over to Crooke and clapped him excitedly on the back, crying, 'Jesus, you got him! You got the bastard!'

Crooke relaxed his grasp on the machine gun and nodded. 'Yes, it looks like it,' he said calmly. He wiped the sweat from his brow and looked down at Mallory. The latter's hands and jacket were thick and greasy with blood as he held the black tie tightly round the wounded gunner's arm. The gunner was now unconscious, his face a heavy grey colour.

Crooke left the gun and went to find 'Revs' who knew where the first aid kit was.

Moments later he picked his way through the shambles and bent over the gunner with the needle. The man's eyes flickered for a moment. He understood and attempted a feeble smile. Swiftly Crooke pressed home the hypodermic. 'Don't worry,' he said with surprising gentleness, 'it'll be all right.'

In the watery blue interior light of the fuselage, the sergeant's eyes filled with what looked almost like love. Then all feeling drained out of him and his pupils rolled upwards. He was unconscious again.

The attack had lasted five minutes at the most, but it had wreaked terrible damage. One engine had gone completely and another threatened to go at any moment. But the pilot was not prepared to abandon his plane. While the survivors tidied up as best they could, the Major brought the Fort down to less than three hundred feet. He hoped that the denser air close to the ground would help keep them airborne; he was pouring every drop of emergency power into the two good engines, while sweating out number one which kept missing a beat every minute.

When they were fifty miles from Cairo, skimming just above the dead-straight coastal road, the pilot ordered the crew to stand by in their parachutes ready to jump if necessary. The sergeant, who had been sick, brought one for Crooke but he turned it down. 'We'll make it,' he predicted, 'and at this height it would be no good anyway.'

Mallory came back to join him and breathed a great sigh as he dropped in the hard seat. 'God, couldn't I just do with a drink and a bath after this!' he exclaimed.

Crooke did not seem to hear him. 'I wonder if we are that valuable,' he said, almost as if he were talking to himself. Mallory looked at him, bewildered. 'What?'

Crooke did not answer immediately. His eyes were fixed on the red warning lights which indicated that the fuel tanks were virtually empty, as the pilot began to lower the flaps prior to landing.

'What struck you about the attack?' he asked after a few moments.

Mallory shrugged. 'What should strike me about it except that it scared the hell out of me?'

'You noted that both planes were fitted with supplementary fuel tanks?'

'Yes, so what?'

'That means they had come a long way. I don't know the range of a Messerschmitt, but let's say three hundred miles.'

Mallory nodded. 'Possibly, but what are

you getting at?'

'Isn't it obvious? They were out looking for us! Canaris's coastal watchers or their Spanish helpers opposite Gib warned the Luftwaffe HQ in Libya that this plane was on its way. Luftwaffe HQ then scrambled their fighters at the nearest base – say Derna. They had a nice little aerial ambush planned for us back there.'

Mallory slowly absorbed the full impact of his statement. The Germans had been forewarned. They knew they were coming and what their mission in Cairo was.

4

Cairo was in a hell of a flap! As they drove through the hot night from the airfield to their quarters, Crooke and Mallory could see that all right. The palm-lined avenues were filled with hundreds of khaki-clad British soldiers, rifles slung over their shoulders, their hair bleached to tow, 'browned off', angry with the heat and the Gippos. Their every gesture seemed to reveal their anger, boredom – and fear; for soon they knew they would be going 'up the blue' to what was waiting for them there.

Once, when they were stopped by a fez-clad policeman, they saw a young soldier knock up a basket of fruit proffered by an Egyptian hawker, sending its contents rolling over the street. 'Bugger off, you wog!' the soldier roared and stamped on a peach. The hawker, frantically gathering up his fruit, was almost in tears but when the soldier was some distance away he stood up, spat, and hurled a stream of harsh guttural Arabic after him.

As their jeep moved away again, Mallory turned to Crooke, who spoke Arabic. 'What did he say?'

'Among other things "You'll soon be running for the Nile, you English dog".'

In the mess that night, toying with their tasteless corned-beef fritters and dehydrated potatoes, the chatter of the staff wallahs was about those who had already fled the capital or were about to go. The rich Egyptians, who had earned a fortune in these last years supplying the Eighth Army, the myriad British civilians who had been on what the bitter staff officers called 'a cushy number' at the various Army headquarters, the many wives of high ranking officers who had infringed regulations to join their husbands

53

working at GHQ – now all of them fought to get on the one train a day which went to Palestine, jeered at and insulted by the skinny Egyptian porters, who would point up to the capital's scavengers, the bronze-brown kites, and cry: 'They'll be waiting for you when the air raids begin!'

But not many Egyptians were fleeing, they learned. Most were waiting confidently for the Germans to come. Even the gross young King, so preoccupied with his pornographic photos and his teenage mistresses, had summoned up enough interest in the war to tell the British Minister, 'When the war's over, for God's sake put down the white man's burden – and go!' And even his direst enemies said that he had no cause for worry. The British would be going even sooner; Rommel would see to that.

As they got into their narrow army cots worn out by the long flight and the air battle, Mallory realized for the first time just how bad the situation in Egypt was. Cairo was a city under siege.

Crooke woke up easily and without effort. Although he had woken once during the night and had been kept awake for some time by the faint noise of the guns at the front, his tiredness had vanished completely. For a moment he stared at the brilliant white light filtering through the cracks in the blackout blind. It was just seven, but already the city was breathless with heat.

The sky was glowing like a furnace. Across the way from the hotel requisitioned by the Army for transients and visitors to GHQ, the Levantine middle-class citizens in the block opposite sat about their balconies in their flowered pyjamas, sweating profusely. Down below the little boys who strung jasmine flowers into necklaces and tried to sell them to the ATS girls who drove trucks daily into the desert to pick up the Eighth Army's dead, were lethargically eating their breakfast saucers of white beans, the peasant's national dish. But as far as he could see, no one was watching their room – yet.

He padded over to where Mallory was sleeping and shook him. 'Time to get up,' he said. 'Our appointment with the GOC is at eight-thirty and he's a stickler for punctuality.'

Mallory groaned. He opened his eyes and closed them again, blinded by the white glare from the window. 'What time are we supposed to meet his nibs – what's his name again?'

'Eight-thirty,' Crooke said firmly, 'and his name is Montgomery.'

Five minutes in the GHQ's great echoing waiting room told them that it too was not free of fear and tension. DRs, covered with desert dust, kept coming and going with their heavy leather pouches. Young staff officers with worried faces continually hurried past, and from a door bearing the old warning poster to 'Keep Mum', a high-pitched voice bordering on the hysterical was saying: 'But I told you, one of our recce patrols damn well saw a group of their officers poking their sticks into the Depression to check if they could run their tanks across. And once Jerry's across that, we're for the high jump.'

Crooke's lean face creased in distaste. 'Typical staff wallah.'

An immaculate young staff captain appeared at the door and announced: 'General Montgomery will see you now.'

If everyone else they had met in Cairo since their plane had landed the previous afternoon had been on edge and tense, the skinny, birdlike man behind the desk seemed to be without nerves. They saluted and he acknowledged the greeting with a nod. He did not smile, but stared at them in the direct disconcerting manner of a child – candid, unhurried and perceptive.

Then in a voice that was as sharp as his nose, he said: 'I have to see you because I have received the Prime Minister's letter. But that doesn't mean I like your visit Commander; or the company you keep. Is that understood?'

'I understand, General,' Mallory answered.

'All right then, you may stand at ease.' He pulled a battered silver watch out of his top pocket and consulted it for a moment.

'Right,' he said, making his 'r' sound like a 'w', 'I can give you exactly two minutes. You'd better tell me what you want.'

He didn't offer them a chair.

'Well, to put it briefly,' Mallory began, 'we have information which leads us to believe that El Nouri Pasha is about to leave us. If I may put you in the picture quickly, it's–'

'You may not,' Montgomery interrupted him. 'Captain Sansom of my own counter-intelligence unit here has given me the details already. I had two minutes with him yesterday.'

'Well, General, my chief, Admiral Godfrey, has been empowered by the PM to see that he doesn't do a bunk. He feels that it's vitally important that Nouri is under constant guard.'

Montgomery looked down at the pile of brown Army forms on his bare desk, as if the interview were already over. He picked up the simple wooden pen of the kind one might find in any rural post office. 'He already is,' he said baldly.

'How, sir?' Crooke spoke for the first time.

'Sansom's got a platoon of MPs posted outside his place. At a discreet distance of course,' Montgomery answered, staring at Crooke as if he were seeing him for the first time.

'But, sir,' Crooke protested. 'MPs hardly measure up to the type of German intelligence operation we expect.'

Montgomery shot him a hard look. 'You are undoubtedly a brave man. But you are a fool and most probably an impertinent one to boot.'

Crooke flushed angrily and Mallory stepped into the breach.

'Honestly, I think Mr Crooke is right, General. They can't be expected to cope with the methods the Jerries will use to get Nouri Pasha out of Egypt.'

Montgomery sighed, as if he fought this type of argument hourly. 'First, Commander, the platoon of MPs is all I have available. Cairo is being drained of anyone capable of holding a rifle for the front. Secondly, even if I had the men, I could not risk flooding the area around Nouri's house with troops. What if he responded by calling out the Egyptian Army? Those young fanatics like Nasser and Sadat would be only too glad to get a crack at us, especially when we're down. They'd be on top of us at the drop of a hat. And we would certainly be in for trouble, serious trouble.' He paused and cleared his throat in that strange manner that Mallory thought seemed peculiar to all generals. 'I must ensure that nothing is done to offend Nouri or his supporters in the Army. Once we have won the battle of Egypt, things will be different. Then I shall deal with General Nouri. But, for the time being, he must be kept sweet. Do you understand, Commander?'

'Yes General,' Mallory said, realizing that there was no further use in protesting.

'Good, then I expect you to be discreet and make do with what is available.' He picked up the wooden pen again, dipped it in the big inkpot and began writing. 'That's all.'

He did not look up as they snapped to attention and saluted. They marched out leaving him working on the plans of the great battle to come.

As the sun hit them outside, Mallory paused and wiped the sweat from his face with a silk handkerchief. 'Not much change there, eh, Crooke?' he said angrily.

'He's a good man,' was Crooke's only answer.

'Do you know what they are saying about him behind his back?'

He repeated the latest piece of malicious GHQ gossip: 'Montgomery is unbearable in defeat, and insufferable in victory.'

But Crooke did not seem to hear. In silence they walked to the waiting jeep.

Half an hour later they arrived at Nouri's house, on the southern outskirts of the capital, where he was being kept under house arrest. The captain in charge of the Military Police squad, who had driven them there, said: 'We'll park here. The Gippo's house is in the next street.'

Mallory nodded in agreement and they walked quickly down the deserted street. The captain stopped at the back door of a rundown villa, the brown stucco peeling off the walls like the leprous symptoms of some loathsome disease. He knocked twice and the door was opened by a big, hard-faced redcap with a broken nose. They were ushered in at once.

The interior was an armed camp. Policemen were everywhere, armed with .38s, stens and rifles. Two World War One Vickers machine guns were set up at each end of the corridor to cover both sides of the house. 'This way, gentlemen,' the MP captain said after the warrant officer in charge had reported that everything was all right. He led them to a darkened room at the front of the villa, where he clicked up the blind and allowed thin strips of light to penetrate the darkness. The temperature went up ten degrees almost instantly. 'Over there,' he pointed, 'the big house with the palms and the two Gippo policemen at the gate.'

Mallory stared out carefully at the silent four-storey building with the two bare-legged, black-uniformed policemen dozing in their boxes outside it; they were obviously the guards. 'Thank you,' he said, and allowed Crooke to take his place.

'The Gippo General bought it in 1920 after he had been accepted into the Gippo Army – you know he fought in the Turkish side against us?'

Mallory nodded.

'For the past year the younger Gippo

61

officers have been using it as their meeting place.' The captain's face wrinkled up in disgust. 'Traitors – the lot of them.'

Crooke turned from the window. 'You've got their photos?' he asked.

The captain showed no surprise at being quizzed in this manner by a junior officer; he had heard of Crooke already. He pointed to the policeman seated by the door, a camera in his hands, which were stained brown with developing fluid. 'He takes them.'

'Do you think El Nouri knows you're here?' Mallory asked.

The redcap shrugged. 'Hard to say. As far as the locals are concerned we're an ordinary MP company which has requisitioned the place as an additional MP post. After all, Cairo is full of deserters and drunks. We do the usual business through the front door during the daytime and out they go by the back door after dark. Of course...'

'Give me your glasses,' Crooke interrupted.

The captain handed them over. Crooke focused them and peered through them with his good eye. Next moment he passed them hurriedly over to Mallory. 'Second floor to the left of the palm. Bathroom window.'

Mallory was just in time to catch a gleam of bright light before it vanished.

'You think the same as I do,' he said a little later as they drove back to their quarters.

Crooke nodded. 'Of course, they've spotted the MPs a long time ago. They've been on to them all the time.'

'So what do we do?'

'It's obvious that the MPs stick out like sore thumbs. We've got to get some additional help.'

'But you heard what Montgomery said,' Mallory protested. 'The barrel of manpower has been scraped clean.'

For the first time since he met Crooke, the latter grinned: 'If you will forgive the pun, Commander, perhaps we need a crook to guard a crook – and where would you find crooks in the Cairo of 1942?' He answered his own question. 'In the glasshouse.'

'The glasshouse?'

'Yes, the same place that Wellington found his best men,' Crooke replied, 'in a British Army military prison.'

5

'Get them knees up... Let's have a bit of movement there!... Now then, you pregnant ducks, swing them arms!... Lef', right, lef', right!'

The harsh voice of the RSM barked out the commands as the men, the backs of their khaki shirts black with perspiration, marched and counter-marched across the burning square of the camp under the midday sun.

'They come here as criminals – we try to make them into soldiers again,' the C.O. of the 54th Base Military Prison explained to Crooke as they stared out at the prisoners from the relative coolness of his darkened office. He touched his Ronald Coleman moustache, as if to reassure himself that it was still there. 'Drill, drill and more drill, that's our motto here.'

Down below a skinny soldier wearing the balmoral of a Scottish Infantry Regiment and the HD divisional patch of the 51st Infantry Division stumbled and sprawled full length in the dust. The RSM was on him in a moment. Halting the column, he ran up to the fallen soldier and poked him in the ribs with his brass-bound pace-stick, bellowing at the top of his tremendous voice so that kites in the trees outside the wire flew off in alarm. 'Get up, you 'orrible, ugly, idle man, you!'

The Commandant smiled in satisfaction and turned to Crooke again. 'We don't believe in mollycoddling them here, you know.'

'Yes, I can see,' Crooke replied, with ill-concealed contempt.

Outside the RSM had grabbed the skinny private by the seat of his shorts and the scruff of his neck and had almost thrown him back into the waiting ranks. 'But I'm not interested in your theories of military re-education. I'm in business for bodies. I need men.'

Captain Reynolds shrugged. 'You're not alone. We get requests every day from the divisions in the line for volunteers. Yesterday, for instance, I sent the 7th Armoured a draft of fifty men serving fifty-six days. Petty stuff. Incorrectly dressed, insubordination and the like. Naturally I don't send them my old lags.' He licked his thick fleshy lips, the sure mark of a sadist or a sensualist, Crooke thought contemptuously. 'They stay here to learn a lesson. They'd be back in here within a few days anyway. No guts, you know. Lack of moral fibre.'

Crooke did not say what he felt. It was easy to talk like that when one was safely ensconced in a nice base job a hundred miles behind the front, subjected to no danger save too much booze and too much rich Egyptian food. 'That's the type I need,' he said coldly. 'The men with the worst records.'

'The worst?' Reynolds repeated, taken aback.

'Yes, Captain. The men who've got nothing to lose. Men who have struck their officers, who have deserted under fire, murderers. You've got murderers, haven't you?'

The Camp Commandant looked at him aghast, his self-assurance gone.

'Well, have you got them or not?' Crooke persisted.

'Of course,' he said hesitantly.

'Good, that's the kind of man I want. With reservations, however. All of them have to be trained, experienced soldiers who've had their whack of service up the blue.'

The Camp Commandant looked at Crooke's face as if he had gone mad, but he remembered the telephone call from GHQ and he didn't want to offend anyone in authority. These days you got sent up the line pretty quickly if you made a balls-up of your job. He opened the window of his office. Burning air flooded in. 'Sergeant-Major,' he bawled, 'Mr Batty!'

Down below the RSM came to a halt. 'Squad,' he roared at the top of his voice, as if the sweating, exhausted prisoners were a mile away instead of a mere ten yards. 'Squaaaad– Halt!'

A hundred pairs of weary feet came to a stop in the ankle-thick dust.

The RSM turned and came to the position of attention. *'Sir?'* he roared.

Crooke had a glimpse of a dark, coarse face, the product of too much brutality and too much beer.

'Get a couple of staffs and bring the prisoners out of the tank,' the Camp Commandant ordered.

'Now, sir?' the gigantic RSM queried.

'Yes, now.'

'Very good, sir.' The RSM whirled round and stamping his highly polished boots went off to find two of the 'staffs', as all the camp's guards were called whether they were staff sergeants or not. Behind him the frightened squad of fifty-six-day men began

67

to sway in the burning sun.

'What's the tank?' Crooke asked while they waited.

Reynolds touched his moustache once more and pointed to a small corrugated-iron structure in the corner of the compound, the heat rippling above the metal roof in blue waves. At each corner there was a small wooden tower containing a 'staff' armed with a Bren gun. 'That's where we keep the trouble-makers. The smart lads who think they can beat the system. The tank teaches them that they can't.' He glanced quickly at his wristwatch, a pompous showy metal-strapped affair. 'At this time of day the temperature under that roof will be anything up to a hundred and thirty.'

Crooke was not a man of great imagination. But he could visualize what it must be like in there, with the water ration limited to two quarts a day and the tin roof above their heads glowing red. With interest, he watched as the RSM, a revolver strapped to his webbing belt now and a pick handle in his hand, followed by two hefty, similarly armed 'staffs' almost as big as himself, started to unlock the big padlock that barred the door.

Men began to stumble out, shielding their blinded eyes from the glare with their arms.

Most of them were clad only in blackened khaki shorts, their bodies greasy with sweat. 'Get in line there, you 'orrible bloody men,' the RSM roared and to emphasize his words he poked their bodies with his pick handle. One of the prisoners hesitated and the RSM hauled back and gave him a great whack with the pick handle across his naked back. It was forbidden to strike prisoners, but out here in the desert the RSM and the Camp Commandant were gods, answerable only to themselves. Who cared about the inmates of the glasshouse and their petty miseries when the whole front was about to collapse?

But the prisoner did not fall. He caught himself just in time and turning to face the man who towered above him said quite clearly in an American accent: 'Do that again, buddy and you won't live to draw your pension.'

The RSM glared at the prisoner but said nothing. The American, a thick red swelling already starting up across his back, staggered after the rest.

'A nice bunch of rogues, eh?' the Commandant commented grimly, as the dozen or so men from the tank formed up in a ragged line under the watchful eyes of the 'staffs'. 'The scum of the British Army. No use to the Army or to society.'

Crooke ignored the comment. 'Tell me about them,' he said, as the RSM chivvied them into rank.

'Well, the man on the left'll be in this office on a charge as soon as you've left,' the Commandant said. 'I won't tolerate that kind of backchat to my NCOs. He's a Yank named Lone Star Alamo Jones.'

He waited for the expected reaction but got none.

'Well, believe me that really is his name. Something to do with his home state of Texas.'

'How did he get in the British Army?'

'He joined us from the Poles in France in '39, after being with the Foreign Legion and before that with the International Brigade in the Spanish Civil War.'

'A communist?' Crooke queried quickly.

The Commandant shook his head. 'No, just a professional soldier-of-fortune.'

Crooke surveyed the American's lean face with the two hard lines that ran down each side of the mouth. He looked a very tough individual indeed. 'What's he in for?'

'Because he is a cold-blooded killer,' the Commandant said vehemently, 'and for insubordination. He was ordered by his CO up the blue to take a collection of very valuable prisoners from the 15th Light Division back for interrogation. When he arrived back at the cage, he was richer by several watches and quite a bit of foreign money. But he was minus the POWs. He'd shot them in cold blood. He got nine years – and was lucky to get away with it.'

'And the next man?'

'Two months ago he got hold of an Arab boy and–'

Crooke cut him short hastily. 'I'm not interested. The next?'

The Commandant's face took on a look of bewilderment as he stared at the next man, who stood rigidly to attention, as if he were on guard outside the Palace, staring at some far object with brown tortured eyes. 'He's a strange one. Sergeant-Major, or rather *ex*-Sergeant-Major Peters of the Coldstream Guards. Holds the DCM and MM with bar.'

Crooke's curiosity was roused. 'What the devil is he doing inside this place?'

'That's the puzzling thing. No one can understand what happened. A regular soldier with a tremendous record. Not one entry in his crime sheet in over eleven years of service in the Army. Brave as they come. Yet two months ago he simply refused to fight anymore. His CO ordered him to take out a patrol and he refused point-blank.'

'Why?'

'As I said, no one knows. His CO tried to reason with him, but failed. They sent him up to Brigade and the Brigadier had a go without success. In the end they ran him back to the medics in Alex, but they failed to get any sense out of him. He simply refused to fight. So the inevitable happened. He was court-martialled. Cowardice under fire. Sentence – five years. And if it had not been for his record, he would have got twice that.'

Crooke looked further down the line of almost naked men sweating in the burning sun, by-passing a plump man who had somehow retained his fat in the hell of the glasshouse. 'The one with the light hair and shirt,' he said. 'That's the "T-T" of the 50th Division patch he's got up, isn't it?'

The Commandant smiled proudly, as if he had achieved something important. 'That's our most famous inmate,' he explained. '*Colonel* Stevens, as the London dailies called him. Y-track Stevens, as everyone up the blue knew him.'

So that was 'Y-track Stevens', a man who had become a legend in the Eighth Army. In '40 he had vanished from his infantry battalion during one of the periodic pull-backs in the desert and had been posted missing, believed dead. But Stevens was not dead by a long chalk. A few months later a Colonel Stevens of the Royal Army Service Corps appeared on Y-track, one of the main arteries leading to the front. The efficient, likeable officer had been in charge of a small RASC unit, which served tea and bully beef sandwiches in a makeshift tented camp to new units on their way up. The place became a recognized stopping point and movement officers planned it into their schedules. Naturally, way out in the desert Colonel Stevens's unit was hard pressed to keep up with supplies and periodically he would have to appeal to unit commanders passing through for whatever they could give him, from razor blades to captured German trucks. Mostly they tried to oblige. Stevens was regarded not only as a supplier of comforts to the men, but also as a rock under fire, ignoring Jerry 'hates', always there under the worst bombardments with a cuppa and a word of cheer for the nervous men going up the line. Indeed, twice he actually rallied broken formations under German attack and prevented the enemy from breaking through.

'When the redcaps finally caught up with him,' the Commandant explained, 'he had a unit of nearly a hundred deserters working for him and was running a regular black market service back to Alex and Cairo with his own fleet of "loaned" three-tonners and captured German vehicles. They said his Cairo bank account ran into thousands.'

'What did he get?'

'Ten.'

The next man was a tall emaciated individual with his head shaved bare to reveal that half his left ear was missing.

'That's Thaelmann.'

'German?'

'Yes, joined the British Army from the Foreign Legion in '40 when the Frogs packed up. Apparently he's been a refugee from Germany since '33.'

'A Jew?'

'No, a communist.'

'What's he here for?'

'Treachery, I suppose you'd call it. He was attached to the Commandos. He and another couple of Germans from the Free French were on a raid and as soon as they hit Jerry lines, the two Germans turned them over to the enemy. Those who got away jumped Thaelmann and took his weapon. There was no evidence that he was implicated, but the powers-that-be thought he would be safer in here than running around loose. He's here indefinitely, until the Legal Branch finds time to have a closer look at the case.'

Crooke looked at his watch. Time was running out. 'The next two?'

'Unnatural practices.'

Crooke waved them aside. 'The tall skinny one with the hooked nose beyond them. Indian Army?'

'No, Egyptian. But a volunteer for the Grenadier Guards.'

'The what?'

'Yes, the Grenadier Guards! And they took him. Ali Hassan Muhammed *Kitchener,* the camp comedian, familiarly known as "Gippo".'

Crooke took a longer look at the tall, skinny half-breed, the only one dressed in a tunic buttoned up to the neck. He noted too the three golden wound stripes decorating his sleeve.

'What's he in for?'

'If only we really knew. Gippo's one of the trickiest customers I've ever come across in three years in this business, I can tell you. His story is that he's Lord Kitchener's grandson. You recollect that Kitchener was out here at the turn of the century. Hence the guards. As he sees it, it's his birthright. In a way he's a remarkable chap for all his tall stories. Speaks fractured English but, as far as I can gather, fluent French, Italian and Arabic and some German. As smart as a whip. But like most Gippos – randy as hell and long fingers.'

He grinned down at the half-breed, standing rigidly to attention in contrast to the slovenly attitude of his neighbours in the line. 'While he was recovering from his third wound in Alex he seduced the wife of the Colonel in charge and nicked her pearls too. Result – five years in here and the threat that the Colonel will shoot him as soon as he sets foot outside that wire.'

Crooke had heard enough. 'All right, Captain, you can dismiss them except the American, Stevens, the big Guardsman, Thaelmann and Gippo. And for God's sake get those men out of the sun!' he pointed to the fifty-six-day men swaying around crazily on the parade ground, still scared enough of the gigantic RSM to be attempting a drunken parody of the position of attention. The Commandant looked annoyed. 'And what do you want with the five?'

76

'I want to see them and I want to see them *alone.*'

'Alone?' the Commandant echoed his statement. 'Are you mad? I'd never see any member of the tank without a couple of armed 'staffs' present. Don't you realize that those men are killers?'

'That is exactly why I want them,' Crooke said calmly.

Crooke stared around at their faces for a moment. Jones, his face non-committal, but his pale yellow eyes sizing up the one-eyed British officer; Y-track Stevens, a wide smile on his cunning Cockney face; Thaelmann, hard and aggressive, the lines of his years of suffering all too evident; Gippo, deep black eyes ingratiating and easy to please; and the Guardsman, his brown eyes completely, utterly blank of any emotion whatsoever.

He picked up the Commandant's silver cigarette case which lay on the desk and passed it round. He knew their ration was one a day. The offer was a deliberate bribe. But only Gippo expressed his gratitude, saying enthusiastically in his fractured English, 'I'm thanking you greatly, sir.'

After they had taken their first grateful drag. Crooke got down to business. 'All right, let me tell you why I'm here. I need

77

some bodies to guard an Egyptian general who is preparing to do a bunk to the enemy.' Swiftly he filled them in while a little green lizard stared down at the strange assembly with a naked, unwinking gaze. 'At present, Nouri is under guard by a platoon of MPs,' he concluded, 'but they're not up to the job.'

'I wouldn't say that, sir,' Y-track Stevens commented cheekily, 'they're not doing so badly in here.'

Crooke ignored the comment. 'The red-caps stick out like a sore thumb. Besides we know that they have been spotted by the Gippos.'

'A very cunning lot of chaps, those wog fellows,' the half-breed remarked, and Crooke saw why the Commandant had called him the camp comedian.

'I need experienced soldiers who can do the job in a different fashion to the redcaps.'

'What's in it for us?' The American spoke for the first time.

'Your freedom. If you volunteer, I have the authority to tear up your crime sheets. You'll be able to make a completely fresh start.'

'Do you think we're fresh off the boat, sir?' Stevens's upperclass 'Colonel's' voice had reverted to its native Cockney. He looked down at Crooke's white knees contemptuously.

'You,' Crooke pointed to Gippo, 'you want to get out of this place, don't you?'

'Yessir, Captain.'

'Good,' Crooke turned and picked up the long document on the desk behind him. 'This is the crime sheet of one Ali Hassan Muhammed Kitchener,' he said, 'known to you as Gippo.' With a quick gesture he tore the brown sheet in half and threw the pieces on the floor. 'Now he's got no record.'

The demonstration had its effect. The American was first off the mark.

'Okay, Lootenant,' he drawled, 'you've got yourself a body.'

Thaelmann snapped to attention. 'I will come too.' Stevens followed. 'Well, if you chaps are going,' he said in his 'Colonel's' accent, 'I suppose I'd better join. The type of person left in the tank is not really my class.'

The rest grinned, save the Guardsman. 'Permission to speak, sir?' he asked in the traditional Guards manner. His accent was pure Geordie.

'Yes.'

'Will there be any killing, sir?'

'I don't know. But I do know I want you.' Selecting his crime sheet from the desk behind him, Crooke tore it up.

'Now you've got to come.'

Then the mood in the Commandant's office relaxed. The ex-prisoner's laughed, as they realized that they were out of the tank at last; even the guardsman seemed at ease. Crooke handed the cigarettes round once more.

He gave them a minute, then he spoke again. 'Your records are now torn up, and you have a chance to make a new start. But don't think you can slip back into your old ways. You have been assigned to my charge and I'm a hard master. And I'm better than you. I know the desert better and I'm tougher. When you're ready to give up, I'll be prepared to carry on just a little bit further. And if any one of you is thinking of going on the trot again, when you're found you won't be returned here anymore. There'll be no more nice military court-martials.'

Slowly he began to take his .38 from its holster. 'I shall be your defence, prosecution – *and judge*. No one cares about your fate. You're the scum of the British Army. The powers that be will be only too glad to forget you ever existed.' He had the pistol out now. From the rafters the lizard was staring at him as curiously as the little semi-circle of ex-prisoners. 'If you desert and I find you again, this is what will happen.'

Without appearing to aim, he pressed the trigger. The lizard fell from the rafters and landed with a soft plop at their feet.

'Mister Crooke, sir!' It was the RSM's thunderous voice from outside. 'You're wanted on the blower! Something's happened back in Cairo. They want you back there *at once!*'

6

'I ought to have tumbled to it at once,' the redcap captain groaned, holding his head with its roughly applied field dressing through which the red stain of his wound was still spreading. 'I bloody well deserve to be put on the carpet for not having spotted what the sods were up to right from the start.'

Commander Mallory looked at the bullet-shattered MP post in dismay. The windows were splintered and the interior walls were pocked with machine gun fire. In the corner eight still, silent shapes lay beneath the rough grey army blankets.

'What happened?' he asked, still tasting the cheap local-made Victory Scotch Whisky, of which he had drunk too much at the local Kit-Kat Club.

'It was just towards the end of midday siesta,' the wounded captain explained, 'when a group of gippos turned up with donkeys. I had a dekko at them, and put them down to the usual hawkers. They start off trying to sell you their ruddy carpets – Persian carpets, made in the next backstreet – and then work their way down to dirty pictures when everything else fails. There were about ten of them working their way down each side of the street from door to door.

'I watched them for a bit, but they looked so genuine, taking their time, giving the servants a lot of lip when they didn't want to buy. In the end I told the men on duty to relax. The situation was normal.'

Mallory took out his hip flask. It was the last of his precious Haig which he had brought with him from London, but he passed it over. 'Have a sip of this,' he said.

The redcap took it gratefully. Behind him they could hear one of the wounded MPs groaning with pain as the MO probed a flesh wound. 'Thanks,' the captain said and handed back an empty flash. Mallory looked at it in dismay.

'A quarter of an hour must have passed by

the time they got level with us,' he went on. 'I happened to glance from behind the blind and caught one taking out his bean bowl and start filling his guts, while one of them with a carpet over his arm came up the path to the front door – there.' He pointed to the shattered door, hanging on its hinges, the wood chipped white with machine gun fire. 'I told the duty man to get rid of him and was about to turn away when the roof fell in. As the duty man opened the door the sod pulled a grenade and lobbed it inside. The duty man let him have a burst in the guts with his sten!' He indicated the skinny brown figure crumpled up in the corner, without benefit of a blanket. 'But two of my lads were killed outright and four bought bad wounds.'

'What then?'

'The men reacted well enough, but they had us pinned down right from the start. Hard bastards they were. They pushed their donkeys down and used them as shields. We could see our bullets hit the poor beasts until they gave up the ghost. Then they let us have it with sub-machine guns. I could spot at least two tommy-guns. God knows where they got them from. There's probably not more than 300 in the whole of the Eighth Army. While they pinned us down, an armoured car drove up. One of our Humbers, armed with a 37mm.'

'An armoured car with British markings?'

'Yes.'

Mallory whistled softly.

'A man in uniform got out and limped across to the door of Nouri's villa. He was a European, I'm sure of that.' Carefully, he released the pressure on his bandage. The blood started to come through again, and he replaced his hold hastily. 'Too tall for a wog and his colour was too light. After he had gone inside the villa the Humber's 37mm opened up on us.' He pointed to the dead donkeys, skinny, ill-treated beasts with their ribs showing through. They lay stretched out stiffly in the road, the white-robed servants from the neighbouring houses gaping at them in open-mouthed awe and the kites hovering overhead waiting for the pickings.

Crooke, who had walked over to the dead Egyptian, said, 'Commander would you come and have a look at this?'

He rolled up the dead Egyptian's sleeve to reveal a muscular arm.

'Well?' Mallory asked.

'Don't you see?'

'No.'

'The vaccination marks?'

'So what?'

Crooke pointed to the man's dusty feet. 'Look at them. They're soft underneath, but calloused at the toes.' He lifted up one foot so that Mallory could see it better.

'Don't you see what it all adds up to?'

'Spare me. I'm not in a mood for playing Sherlock Holmes.'

'Well I'll spell it out for you. This man is no ordinary hawker. He's been vaccinated for one thing. He's too well fed – look at that arm. And for years he's been wearing shoes whereas most of the peasants are barefoot. Or I should say boots because of the hard flesh. *Army boots,* in short.'

'You mean he was in the Egyptian Army?'

'Yes. Where else would they have got the armoured car from?'

'My God, if they've got him…' He didn't finish his sentence.

'I've got to get to a phone. We've got to warn all fields to watch out for any attempt to fly Nouri out.'

'No need, Commander.' The wounded captain raised his blood-stained head. 'I didn't make a total balls-up of it, after all. Naturally they cut the wires of our phones and the rest of them down the street. But they hadn't reckoned with our short wave transmitter in the jeep at the back. I got on to Heliopolis field first, and then on to RAF Headquarters. I passed the word on. Every Gippo plane throughout the Delta has been grounded. In essence, the whole Gippo Air Force is hors de combat until we give the word that they can fly again – and RAF HQ is patrolling each field with its planes in case anyone tries to take off illegally.'

Mallory breathed a sigh of relief. 'Good man,' he said, 'but nevertheless, if they planned so hard to get Nouri out of the villa, they've obviously got a scheme to get him out of Cairo – if they haven't got him out already. The question is how they're going to get him to the Germans. Nouri is a tough old boy, but he's nearly sixty and he couldn't face the trip through our lines on foot, a vehicle would never get through.' He tried to imagine what the men who had abducted him would do now.

Crooke turned to the captain. 'You mentioned a European getting out of the Humber. Can you describe him more clearly?'

'I only saw him for a second. When that 37mm started firing, I didn't stop around to gawp exactly. But the impression I got was that he was tall and skinny – and he was a

European, and as I said before, he limped.'

'You're sure of that?'

'Yes.'

'Then think carefully. Can you remember with which foot he limped?'

The redcap stood up painfully. He pushed out his left foot and then pulled it back. 'He got out of the Humber and dropped to the ground. I heard the clang as the gunner closed the turret hatch behind him. Then he set off inside the villa – on the right foot.'

'*Right* foot?'

'Yes, I'm sure. I must have registered that a soldier would have set off with his left. So he must have dragged his left.'

'That's what I thought,' said Crooke and turned to Mallory. 'Come on, we've got to get going!'

'Where to?'

'To meet my command!'

Crooke had deposited the five ex-glasshouse inmates at the Cairo Citadel which stands on the edge of the desert, where the Muquatim slopes down towards the Nile. It had been an obvious choice, for the Citadel housed the HQ of his former unit, the Long Range Desert Group. Not too many questions would be asked by the permanent staff or by the few patrollers fitting out again for another six-week stint in the desert. In addition to which there was plenty of special equipment there which he might need before he was finished.

While Crooke had been questioning the wounded captain they had been equipping themselves. Now they faced Crooke and the Commander, shaved, hair trimmed and dressed in relatively new shirts and shorts.

Gippo pulled out the silver cigarette case which a few hours before had graced the glasshouse commandant's desk. 'Oh, by the way, Admiral,' he remarked, 'I have been finding this.'

Mallory grinned but didn't take the proffered case. 'All right, now get this. Mr Crooke has filled you in, I know. But the situation has changed radically since he spoke to you. The man you were to guard has legged it. Now you are going to find him.'

'Where?' the American asked sizing up the Commander, toying all the while with an ugly Colt .45 which he had got from somewhere or other.

'Questions later, listen first,' Mallory snapped.

The American's face curled into an ill-concealed sneer, as he gazed at Mallory's knees.

Mallory felt himself go a bit red. 'One day,' he promised himself, 'I'll fix you for that, Mr Bloody Lone Star Alamo Jones!' But he kept his temper. 'All we know at the moment is that he can't get out of Egypt by crossing our lines on foot. He's too old for that. We've already blocked the air routes. And if he tried to pass through our lines around Alamein by vehicle, we'd nab him. So, whoever's got him will try to get him out by doing a left hook and swinging through the border between Egypt and Libya via the desert; you'd better tell them that part, Crooke.'

Crooke pointed to the large scale map of Egypt on the wall behind him. 'There are two back doors to Egypt or to Libya whichever way you look at it. You follow the route south-west past the Giza pyramids. Two days later you are at Ain Dulla, a small oasis on the eastern fringe of the Great Sand Sea. There you turn due west, where you face what Major Clayton called, many years ago, the "Easy Ascent".' He indicated a spot in the sparsely marked area of southern Egypt. 'It's a great curving ramp of sand running up to the summit of a rock wall. Now it's probably in a bit of a mess because previous Long Range Desert Patrols have churned up the sand and the ascent is not easy anyway – in spite of the name. But it can be done. In fact, our people do it every three weeks or so on their way into Libya.'

He paused to let his words sink in. The others remained silent, their eyes glued to the great white emptiness of the map below the Easy Ascent. 'Once you're through the narrow rock ridge between two very deep gullies, you're through to the Great Sand Sea and the back door is open.' He paused again, then after a moment he said slowly, 'There is another way.' He pointed to the end of the Great Sand Sea, perhaps five hundred miles farther south, deep into the desert. 'This is the end of surveyed territory. But we do know there is a sort of mountain range, which might be passable because the rock would offer traction for vehicles.'

'But nobody has ever been down there, sir!' It was Gippo. 'I am living in this country since many years now. And the wogs they tell me that.'

Crooke nodded in agreement. 'That's true – or almost true. I've never been that far myself, and my knowledge is merely hearsay. The terrain is supposed to be murderous according to Bagnold. But there was some-one who did get that far.' Mallory frowned. He hoped that Crooke's fascination for the desert was not going to sidetrack him. Time was of the essence. Every hour counted and he could not tolerate Crooke wasting it with his half-baked desert lore.

But Crooke did not see the frown. He continued speaking, almost as if the others were not there, his one bright blue eye fixed on some distant object. 'In 1937 the Anglo-Egyptian Geographic Society sent out a survey team to try to map the area. It was led by an Egyptian and a British officer. He was Colonel Youngblood of the Guards. The Egyptian was Hassan Nouri.'

'The son of the man we're looking for?' Mallory asked.

Crooke nodded. 'But there was a third man, a professional cartographer, an Austrian-Hungarian, who surprisingly enough, had fought in the desert with the Turks against Youngblood in 1917. A man named Kun – Count Kun. By all accounts he was an impoverished Central European aristocrat who after losing his family estates following the Great War came to Egypt and joined the survey. He wasn't just a cartographer. He was an amateur archaeologist, who had a bee in his bonnet about finding the lost oasis of the Persian King Cambyses who sometime in the fifth century before Christ went mad after he conquered Egypt and according to some accounts disappeared deep into what is now the desert. Why he wanted to find it, no one knows. But at all events the three of them, the British soldier, the young Egyptian and the mysterious Austrian Count were a strange trio and inevitably they started quarrelling.'

He cleared his throat. 'In the desert it is easy to start a fight. The suspicion that one member of the party is getting a couple of drops of water too much or an easier position when you're trying to push your vehicle out of the sand, the best bit of shade underneath it – any of those things can turn a person, a normally law-abiding person, into a savage killer. Out there in the desert reactions are like the primary colours, stark black and white – none of your northern European greys. When the going got almost impossible and supplies started to give out, the three leaders pushed on alone, leaving the rest of the convoy to make their way back to the nearest oasis. When the convoy eventually reached Cairo they reported to El Nouri that the Englishman had deliberately forced his son to push on. And that was that. No more was heard of the three and the death of his only son not only turned El Nouri fanatically anti-British, but pushed him into the camp of the young rebel officers. No one ever found out what happened to the leaders. Bagnold tried in '38, but had to turn back when the springs of his truck broke. It remains a mystery why they were determined to push on in spite of their lack of supplies and the Austrian's physical difficulties.'

'Physical difficulties?' Mallory interrupted.

'Yes; in the Great War he had been wounded; it left him with a bad limp in his left leg.'

Mallory stared at him open-mouthed, while the glasshouse inmates gazed at the two officers in bewilderment. At last the Commander broke the silence. 'While you were at the military prison, Field Security phoned to say that the footprints of the man who got away from the seaplane showed that he limped badly – with the left foot.'

7

Mallory did not see much of Crooke and his men in the next twelve hours. Twice he offered aid, but his help was not needed so after staring disconsolately at the view from the Citadel, which took in Cairo, the Pyramids and the edge of the desert, he returned to his quarters. But he could not sleep in spite of his fatigue. Perhaps it was the thick heat. More probably, he thought, it was the knowledge that Kun, the mysterious Austrian, had already set out on his long journey into the desert. In the end he gave up trying to sleep and took himself off to the Kit-Kat Club, its Victory Whisky and its belly dancers. But even when Hekmath, the star of the show, thrust her admirable pelvis invitingly in his direction, he could not forget Crooke and his efforts to fit out a truck to take up the chase into the unknown. Would he be able to pull it off in time? Over and over again, Mallory found himself clenching his fists with tension. Hekmath's generous curves did nothing to distract his mind from the question which nagged persistently at his mind. Could Crooke do it?

In August 1942, it was difficult to get spare equipment in besieged Cairo; anything available was being shipped to the front by Montgomery, who was a traditional Great War General in the sense that he wanted overwhelming material superiority before he engaged in battle. But Crooke, like most of the Long Range Desert officers, was an expert at 'official' scrounging. Through an old connection, he got the Chevrolet Company in Alex to let him have the last of their special thirty-hundredweight trucks, equipped with Egyptian Army sand tyres.

Swiftly he and his ex-lags, as he called them, went to work to strip it down, ripping off doors, windscreens and hoods. At the same time the guardsman and the equally silent Thaelmann, an excellent mechanic, combining German thoroughness with transatlantic speed, set about strengthening the truck's springs. Meanwhile, the American got busy fixing the special mountings for the vehicle's three machine guns, a brand-new 50 inch Browning against air attack and two Great War vintage Lewis guns to be fixed over the windscreen in the seat next to the driver. For the first time since he had been released from the tank, Crooke could see a look of animation on the man's thin face. 'Boy,' he muttered over and over again, as he worked at fitting the guns, 'what beauts!'

But if Crooke had little difficulty in getting the vehicle and the weapons, he found that official doors were closed when he asked for other supplies. His old reputation before the Rommel raid and what had happened in

London had caught up with him. In spite of his authorization from the head of Naval Intelligence, officialdom met him with a fake smile and a firm no. 'You're bad news, old boy, you see,' as one more friendly staff officer explained, after he had been refused a ration of petrol for the tenth time. *'The powers-that-be don't want to know you.'*

In the end he put the problem to Gippo and Stevens who had been doing some fairly enterprising scrounging in the Citadel itself. 'Blimey, Mister Crooke,' Stevens said, 'why didn't yer give me the wire before.' He nudged a grinning Gippo. 'Come on you filthy hairy nig-nog, you, let's see what Colonel Stevens can do.' And after dumping the 'borrowed' navigation equipment and sand channels for unsticking vehicles, they took off for Cairo.

Gippo came back two hours later, driven up by a bespectacled American colonel with a jeep full of jerry cans. While the rest unloaded the petrol, the Colonel, who had a pale innocent face and explained to Crooke he had just got off the plane to join the Embassy's military staff, twirled the Luger for which he had exchanged the petrol happily and explained exuberantly: 'By Golly, I wonder what the folks back in Wichita will say when they hear I've got Rommel's own pistol. Hot dog, ain't that just something!' Crooke agreed it was and looked across at Gippo. Gippo looked away tactfully.

Stevens took longer to get back. The sun was a blood-red semi-circle on the desert horizon when he came driving up to the workshop where the rest of them still laboured with oil-grimed, sweaty faces. He was driving a huge gleaming staff car. 'Get them doors closed – *quick!*' he snapped through the window and without waiting for them to ask questions drove in at them.

'What the hell ya got there, Stevens?' the American asked.

Stevens waited by the six seater Daimler till the big corrugated iron doors were closed. He winked conspiratorially. 'A little gift from GHQ,' he announced.

Even Crooke was taken aback by the Cockney's audacity. 'My God, where did you say, Stevens?' he asked.

'I can tell you,' the guardsman said and pointed to the flag on the bonnet.

'Christ, I forgot that! No wonder them redcaps saluted when I went through the gates of the POL depot and asked 'em to give me the jerry cans,' Stevens said. He pointed to the back seats. They were piled

97

high with 5 gallon cans of fuel. 'I told 'em the Corps Commander needed it for going up the blue.'

'Good man,' Crooke said briskly. 'But for God's sake, let's get it unloaded and the car back to Cairo before the MPs come looking for us.'

By midnight they were about finished. The khaki-coloured 'Chevvy' was piled high with supplies, ammunition, bedrolls and personal effects. Mallory and Crooke checked through each item singly. A mistake in the number of jerry cans filled with water or even a missing item as small as a bag of salt tablets, so vital in the intense heat, could spell disaster in the desert. Slowly but surely they worked through the gear, which contained such items as tins of Eno's Fruit Salts to add to stale water to make it potable.

Now and again Crooke looked at his watch and muttered angrily, 'Where are they?'

'Who?' Mallory queried as he counted through the heavy sheepskin overcoats; in the desert the nights and mornings were often intensely cold.

'Stevens and Gippo. I told them to take back the Daimler.'

'You don't think they've done a bunk, do you?'

'It's not likely. I think I can trust them.'

They finished their count and Crooke announced that there was cold Rheingold beer in the ice-chest for those who wanted it. While they settled down to the beer, Mallory pulled out a bottle of Victory Whisky and handed it to Crooke. 'Take a pull, I brushed my teeth this morning – I think.'

Crooke shook his head. 'No thank you. I prefer to do without.' Mallory did not pursue the subject; he knew that he was utterly dependent on Crooke now.

'If your Count has indeed got Nouri and is trying to get him out in the manner you suggest, where do you think he will rendezvous with Rommel's men?'

'You remember the El Kharga Oasis on the map?'

Mallory nodded.

'El Kharga is the last place held in the south by a mixed force of Egyptians and British troops. Of course we can't rely on the Egyptians to help us. But I've radioed the British commander to keep his eye on the situation. Personally, however, I don't think they'd rendezvous there. Too chancy. My guess is it'll be beyond El Kharga, somewhere in the desert. I'd hazard...'

A sudden crash killed the rest of his sentence. The door flew open and a skinny terrified Egyptian in a dirty white robe flew in, sprawling at Crooke's feet. Behind him stood a grinning Gippo, a long wicked-looking commando knife gripped in his thin bony hand.

'Dirty wog!' he cried, 'listening at the doorknob.'

Stevens appeared behind him. 'Caught him hanging around at the window, sir,' he said.

'Yes, wasn't you!' Gippo snarled and hit the Egyptian across the face. Mallory heard the big ring Gippo had suddenly acquired strike home. Blood welled up from the man's hook-nose as Gippo dragged him to his feet.

The Egyptian let loose a long stream of terrified Arabic.

'We was delayed, sir,' Stevens explained. 'They didn't want to pay our price for the Daimler.'

Mallory repressed a groan. This gang of old lags would have him behind bars if they kept on like this.

'Just as we were sneaking in past the sentries – we didn't want them to know we'd been out, no names, no packdrill, you know – we saw this horrible object listening in.'

'Let him go,' Crooke commanded. Gippo relinquished his hold, but kept the knife at the ready. 'Do you speak English?' he asked.

The Egyptian's eyes rolled eloquently.

Gippo snarled at him in Arabic.

'Aw, give him me,' the American chipped in. 'I'll soon make him into a singing tenor.'

'No, leave it to me,' Crooke ordered. 'If he doesn't talk in exactly thirty seconds, you can have him, Jones.'

Suddenly the terrified spy found his tongue. In broken but fluent English, he blurted out his story. A man had approached him on the street... Yes, an Egyptian, an effendi... He had given him pounds, five... He must find out what the one-eyed English in the Citadel was doing... As soon as he knew when they were to set out ... then he should report to the headquarters of the Seventh Infantry Battalion... There the commander would give him money ... five pounds more. The spy fell on his knees, his hands raising in the classic pose of supplication.

Crooke drew his revolver slowly.

Mallory stared at him. 'What are you going to do?'

'We want no witnesses,' Crooke answered.

'Permission to speak, sir?' It was the guardsman. His face wore a look of intense outrage. 'Is there no other way? Hasn't there been enough killing?'

Crooke ignored him. Slowly he raised the revolver. 'We want no witnesses to our departure. What else can we do with him? If we turn him into the Central Guardroom the enemy would know we'd left Cairo within the hour.'

'But sir,' the guardsman pleaded, grabbing Crooke's arm, 'you've got to give him a chance! You...'

The Egyptian leaped forward. There was a knife in his hand. A sudden crack. A whiff of cordite. The Egyptian took the bullet in the small of his back. A hole appeared in his dirty robe. Slowly, his knees buckling under him, he sank to the floor. Behind him, Thaelmann, his face as impassive as ever, said, 'A fool – a mere pawn,' and put away his .38.

The others looked at him, only half understanding. Then they looked down at the wounded man, sprawled on the floor, the knife still grasped in his skinny brown hand.

Almost casually Crooke stepped over him. Before Mallory or the guardsman could stop him, he bent down and placed his revolver two finger widths above the right eyebrow. With a slight intake of breath, he squeezed the trigger. There was another shot, muffled a little this time. The Egyptian's body jumped violently. His spine arched. Then it crashed down again. There wasn't much of his head left.

It was just before dawn and the red disc of the sun had not yet nudged its way across the silent black horizon. The desert before them was still clothed in darkness. The sky above their heads, as they smoked their last cigarettes, was a dirty whitewash. Everything was silence, disturbed only by a faint breeze from the sand. Commander Mallory yawned.

'Well Crooke it's time, isn't it?'

Crooke drew on his sheepskin coat. At this time of night, the cold penetrated to the very bone. 'Yes, I suppose it is.'

Mallory put out his hand. 'Crooke, let me wish you luck.'

Crooke took it. 'Thank you.' He turned and walked over to the waiting crew. 'Cigarettes out,' he ordered softly.

'You can start up, Thaelmann.'

'You'll bring him back, Crooke,' Mallory shouted.

'I will,' he shouted back. 'OK, let's go.'

Thaelmann let out the clutch. The Chevvy drew away smoothly and picked up speed on the white tarmac road. The gate loomed up but the sentry opened the barrier long before the truck got there. It moved through without slowing down, and then it was gone.

For a moment Mallory stood there alone in the icy pre-dawn air, hardly realizing that he was shivering with cold. They were off at last, on a mission that was little short of impossible – trying to find a single individual somewhere in thousands of square miles of desert, some of it uncharted, with only themselves to rely on. 'A strange bunch,' he said half aloud, 'a ruddy strange bunch.'

As he crossed the deserted square, which had seen generations of British soldiers bashing its surface with their big black boots, he started to compose his daily signal. It would begin: '30.8.42 AM. ON THIS DAY MALLORY'S DESTROYERS COMMENCED MISSION...'

TWO: INTO THE DEVIL'S COUNTRY

'There are not many men who are prepared to enter the devil's country. But there are a few of us who have always been fascinated by it. Apart from the war itself, down there is the last challenge.'
2/Lt Crooke to Commander Mallory

1

The first day was easy. The road was good, only occasionally drifted over with shifting sand, and, as the sun started to go down, they reached a small Anglo-Egyptian military encampment, where they took a couple of turns down the one and only road to make everyone aware that they were there. They then filled up at the local RASC POL depot, ate a quick meal of fried bully and tinned peaches and bedded down for the night.

At three, the guardsman who had the last hour's 'stag' wakened them all gently. Softly they rose to their feet – they were already fully dressed, apart from their boots and at Crooke's command began pushing the truck out of the still-sleeping camp. They pushed it for nearly two hundred yards until they came to a long incline. Quickly Thaelmann shoved home the gear and the rest jumped aboard as the truck began to gather momentum. Crooke cast a glance behind them. There was no sign of life from the Egyptian camp. They hadn't been spotted. The motor came to life almost without noise.

That day the road gave out and was replaced by a track. But the sand was firm and apart from a couple of soft patches, the going was good. Two days out they by-passed the small oasis of Ain Dulla, on the eastern fringe of the Great Sand Sea. When they were safely away from the place, which might well have held a small Egyptian Army garrison, Crooke ordered them to brew up while he took a compass reading. Half an hour later he ordered Thaelmann to drive due west, heading for the well-remembered 'Easy Ascent'. They bedded down that night some fifty miles away from the ridge.

They started next morning just before dawn. The wind was bitterly cold and flung particles of sand like ice against their faces. They were glad of the warmth of the sheepskin coats. Before them stretched lines and ever more lines of dunes, sweeping on to the far horizon. Some were rolling, but more were razor-backed and Crooke knew from experience that it took a very special kind of driver to master them, but Thaelmann, taking turns with the equally skilled and silent guardsman, was obviously no amateur. Both were excellent drivers with an eye for the ground and both could spot a soft area as quickly as Crooke himself. Thus, after his attempts at advice had been met by a grunted '*Ja*' on the part of the German or a muttered 'yessir' from the guardsman, he gave up and let them get on with it.

Thaelmann proved particularly good at tackling the razor-backed sand dunes; he had the special techniques at his finger tips. He would position the Chevvy horizontally to the dune, accelerate at top speed and then shortly before they lurched alarmingly over the top – possibly to be faced by a drop of twenty or thirty feet – he would swing the wheel round violently and roll down the opposite side at a hair-raising angle.

But even his skill could not prevent the heavily-laden vehicle from being bogged down at least once an hour. Then everyone had to grab a shovel and begin the back-breaking, time-consuming business of digging the heavy wheels free so that sand channels could be placed underneath.

On that second afternoon they hardly made twenty miles and the temperature was unbelievable. The sand, too, plagued them. In spite of their goggles and face cloths; it penetrated everywhere – mouth, ears, eyes, all over the body so that they scratched themselves raw in the heat. At night they fell into an exhausted sleep, neglecting even to brew up the precious 'char'.

Crooke woke about two. It was the noise, the well-remembered desert noise. Above him, as he lay there his hands propped under his head, the night was brilliant. The stars were harsh and silver in the sky, so close it seemed one could reach up easily and grab one. And all around him he heard the old, old sound – the singing of the sand. The millions of sandgrains which contracted at night due to the cold were now moving, rubbing against one another, giving out a strange haunting music.

For what seemed a long while he lay there, planning the next day and wondering if his scheme would come off – it was his only chance of making a quick contact. Then he heard a soft cough from the front seat of the Chevvy. He looked across. It was Peters. Ever since they had left the Citadel, he had always seemed to land this middle of the night hour for his spell of 'stag'. Crooke looked at his watch. Another two hours before dawn.

Suddenly, on instinct, he unzipped his sleeping bag and, shuddering a little with the cold, pulled on his boots and walked across to the guardsman. He attempted to rise, but Crooke motioned him not to move. He slipped in beside him, behind the twin Lewis guns. As sentries were not allowed to smoke at night in the desert – their glowing cigarette ends could be seen for miles off on the plain – he reached in his pocket and pulled out a handful of boiled sweets taken from their Compo ration box. 'Take a couple,' he said, tendering them.

'Thank you, sir,' the guardsman said warily.

Above them a shooting star undertook a short but spectacular dive towards the earth.

'When did you join the Army, Peters?' Crooke asked.

'Thirty-one, sir. I was three years on the dole. Jobs were hard to come by then in Durham. As soon as I was old enough I enlisted in the Coldstream.'

'Why the Guards?'

'Up there the Coldstream is almost like a county regiment. It was hard at first; you know the Brigade, sir. But for me in those days it was like paradise after the dole and hand-outs at the workhouse. Three square meals a day and all found. You couldn't beat it. Three months after I'd left the depot, we were in India too, getting our knees brown for the first time. That was something for a lad from a Durham council school, I can tell you. That did it for me. I'd found a home in the Army, as they used to say on the recruiting posters. I was lance-sergeant by '39, Company sergeant-major by '41, out here.'

He hesitated and Crooke coaxed him on: 'What went wrong?' he asked.

The guardsman wiped his brow, as if he were warm, although the temperature was in the low thirties. 'It's hard to explain, sir. First, most of the old officers had bought it. We got green lads from the UK to replace them, and they never lived long enough to get any experience. A year ago today, we lost a company in one afternoon because of that. I started to feel I'd had enough. All those big lads stretched out on the sand. Then all the back and forth, sir. I don't know how to explain it really. But it seemed as if it would never end. It was all for nothing. It seemed to me that my lads were going for a Burton for no purpose. All the killing didn't bring us one bit closer to finishing the whole bloody business.' He caught his anger in time, in the manner of the good CSM he had once been. 'I decided I'd had enough.' His voice trailed away. 'I didn't want to kill any more, get anybody else killed because of my orders...'

For a while they sat there in silence. Around them the sand shifted back and forth. Underneath the truck Thaelmann was snoring softly.

'I understand,' Crooke said, breaking the silence. 'I understand well enough. This desert war has gone on far too long. We've got to put an end to it – *soon*.'

'*We*, sir?' the guardsman asked. 'What can we do? It's up to the brasshats, and we know what they've been like in the past!'

'That's it, Peters! We need new thinking in this war if we're going to win it. Those staff wallahs back in Cairo are still thinking in terms of trench warfare. Mass action by thousands of men, all arranged according to timetables, startlines and the rest of the nonsense. What we need is ruthless, small-party actions. Give me a platoon of tough, well-trained men, who play rough and play to win, and I'd tackle – *and beat* – any conventional infantry battalion.'

In the icy light of the stars, the guardsman could see the officer's single blue eye glitter.

'What will you do this time?' Crooke asked softly.

'How do you mean, sir?'

'You know what I mean!' He indicated the rifle. 'What will you do when you have to fire that again?'

The guardsman hung his head like a small child, caught dipping his finger into the jampot. 'I don't know, sir, I honestly don't know.'

Five minutes later Crooke walked back to his bedroll. Taking off his boots he clambered inside. He closed his eyes. For a while he hung on. Once he heard a whispered exchange between Peters and Stevens. Then sleep began to take hold of him. Just before he fell asleep, he thought he heard the faint sound of a truck starting a long way off, but he might have been mistaken, he told himself. A moment later he was gone.

Next morning they set off again, still heading west. The country began to change. The flat sand, interrupted by the killing sand dunes, gave way to a rough broken terrain made up of flat-topped hills. Their progress accelerated. Leaving Thaelmann in complete charge of the driving, Crooke concentrated on the country ahead, his one eye searching the horizon. But there was nothing to be seen.

At midday he ordered a halt. It had been a long, hot morning and they needed no urging. Stiffly but hurriedly, Stevens, who, with Gippo, had taken over the cooking, dropped from the truck and pulled out the blackened can over which they cooked.

Gippo scooped up sand and filled the bottom of the can to a depth of three inches. Then he fetched a jerry can of petrol and a pint of the precious fuel was drawn off. He poured it into the sand while Stevens stirred the mixture to the consistency of porridge. Satisfied, he rose to his feet and said, 'Get downwind, Gippo, and move the jerry can.'

Stevens then lit a match and dropped it into the can. There was a soft whoosh and the sand began to burn. Their oven was ready for the first dixie of canned M & V, the standard component of their compo ration- meat and vegetable stew.

Crooke watched them for a moment. Then he walked over to the truck, grabbed a handful of Army Form Blank and a shovel. He strode towards the nearest flat hilltop, the spade in one hand, the paper in the other. On the far side he would find a concealed spot. He felt an unpleasant movement in his guts, and hoped he was not in for a case of the squitters.

As he breasted the hilltop all worries on that account vanished abruptly. There in the wadi below, he saw the tracks. His first instinct was to drop the spade and run down to examine them but he caught himself just in time. Instead he loosened his belt and squatted down, surveying the tracks. When he was finished, he took the spade and started to cover the faeces, but his eyes were examining the number, the depth and the direction of the tracks all the time. Finally he was satisfied. He turned and walked back to the vehicle.

Stevens was already beginning to dole out the M & V. He caught sight of Crooke and nodded to Gippo. 'Come on, you filthy nig-nog! Can't yer see the officer's waiting for his grub.'

Hastily Gippo presented Crooke with his share. 'Here you are, sir,' he said ingratiatingly, 'very special today, sir. I have been putting a little bit of wild garlic in it.' His black eyes twinkled. 'Very spicy, very good for jig-jig.'

Crooke thanked him, amused, as Stevens stirred up the sand in the can and put on a dixie of water. 'Char'll be up in a brace of shakes,' he said and sat down to eat his stew.

Crooke let them eat in peace. If they were being watched, he told himself, the best thing was to act normally. He let them finish their char before he gave out his orders. 'Before we leave here, I want each one of you to check his weapons.'

'That'll take the cowboy a couple of hours at least,' Stevens cracked, pointing to the American, who, in addition to his original Colt, had already picked up a tommy-gun and a wicked-looking German Schmeisser pistol. 'He's got enough popguns to start a private army.'

'Aw, go and crap in ya hat,' the Texan snapped back.

Crooke let them laugh for a moment. Then he gave them his second order. 'And every man is to take a couple of sandbags from the truck and fill them up with sand too before we leave.'

'Sandbags, sir?'

Crooke nodded but he did not give any explanation.

Half an hour later they set off again. Crooke took his seat beside Thaelmann. Everything seemed to be going according to plan.

2

The big overladen yellow truck came grinding up a steep incline in second gear, a long cloud of dust trailing far behind it. The horizon was breaking up into dirty white streaks. Soon it would be dark. Already the high plateau behind them was a stark black outline against the sky. Yassa tightened his grip on the field glasses as he watched them come.

'I should like to take my bren,' the sergeant hissed as he crouched next to Yassa on the rock, 'and explode it in their faces. I hate them.'

'Be quiet,' Lieutenant Yassa said softly. The NCO was like all the Delta people – hysterical, loud and given to a lot of hot-headed talk. But when it came to action, then they were not so eager.

Yassa, the descendant of Turkish beys who had ruled Egypt before the French and British came, adjusted his binoculars carefully, taking care that some odd gleam from their lenses did not betray his platoon's position among the rocks. There were six of them, just as Cairo had radioed him two days before. Next to the driver a man jerked rhythmically to every bump that the truck went over. He appeared to be asleep. Yassa hoped so. Those two Lewis guns in front of him looked damned dangerous. Behind, the other four were similar dark outlines, jogged up and down by the motion of the vehicle labouring up the slope. They were asleep too.

The Chevvy was getting close now. He would give them four hundred before he ordered the platoon to open fire. He looked around quickly at the twenty or so men sprawled among the rocks, their rifles aimed at the approaching truck, and changed his mind. He'd better play safe; most of them were poor shots. He would wait until the enemy was three hundred yards away.

Yassa picked up the rifle that the Germans had dropped in the last para consignment. It was a fine weapon. He sighted it on the rock, which he had set himself as a marker. The truck was almost up to it now.

'All right,' he commanded softly. 'Take it calmly. Don't fire too high. I shall take the man with the guns next to the driver. Sergeant, you take the truck. The rest of you aim at the men at the back among the baggage. You understand?'

The men, in their ill-fitting robes, with which Sadat had equipped them at their regimental depot nodded.

As he slipped off the safety catch, Yassa told himself it would be up to him. If he could knock out the soldier behind the Lewis guns before he could get them into action, the platoon would be all right. But once they started firing back, his men would break. It was as simple as that. One must not fool oneself about the fighting qualities of the Delta people.

Carefully Yassa prepared to fire. The rifle was beautifully balanced, far superior to the old American Ross or Lee Enfield which was all the English would allow the Egyptian Army. He tucked the butt firmly into his shoulder and brought the sight to bear on the man next to the driver. He was still hunched up as if asleep. Yassa's finger curled round the trigger. The white blur of the man's face filled the cross wires of the sight. The man was definitely asleep, the white blur bumping up with every pothole awkwardly. 'Soon, my friend,' he muttered grimly, 'you will sleep forever.' He gritted his teeth beneath the thin moustache and pressed the trigger. The rifle kicked back against his shoulder. A solitary shot rang out across the silent desert.

For a long moment nothing happened.

Then the Englishman slumped forward against the guns, as if propelled by some invisible hand. The platoon let loose a volley of ragged fire, which developed into a orgy of wild shooting.

'The pigs, the English pigs!' yelled the sergeant beside Yassa and squeezed the trigger of the Bren.

Sand spurted up a dozen yards away from the truck.

'Up your sight, you fool!' Yassa shouted angrily.

But some of their bullets were hitting the truck and obviously they had achieved complete surprise. As the truck ground on in second gear, the driver, his body protected by that of the man slumped next to him, frantically tried to reach the top of the incline, the figures in the back of the vehicle slumped forward one after the other, dead or dying.

Then suddenly, the truck started to pick up speed. The driver, crouched over his wheel, had obviously found a patch of firm sand on the incline. Another fifty yards and he would make it! Desperately Yassa raised his rifle. He had no time to take careful aim and the dead man was in the way. He fired once and the driver slumped forward over his wheel. But somehow or other, he kept his foot down on the accelerator. In his moment of death he kept on driving.

'Cease fire!' Yassa yelled.

Gradually the firing died away.

'We've got them,' the sergeant cried jubilantly, 'we've got them!'

'Be quiet, you fool,' Yassa commanded. He got to his feet and watched the truck still moving at perhaps 20 kilometres an hour, getting ever closer to the darkness coming in from the high plateau. He shuddered suddenly. A mobile coffin carrying the dead English into the shades. While the awed soldiers watched curiously, he debated with himself whether he should order his own vehicle after it. Then he decided not to. He knew his white-livered, superstitious Delta people; if they were forced to spend this night with the English dead, they would be awake half the time and seeing ghosts all the way back to Cairo.

Finally the darkness swallowed up the truck, though they could hear its motor faintly for a little while longer. Then it was gone altogether. Yassa turned and looked at his men. Their jubilation at their victory had vanished altogether; they looked scared. God, he thought to himself in contempt, what rats they are.

But when he spoke, his voice revealed nothing of his feelings.

'You,' he nodded to the sergeant, 'get on the radio and contact the German. Tell him we have carried out the operation – *successfully...*'

Against the star-studded sky that hid the featureless plain in front of them, the six trucks were outlined by the flickering light of the camp fires. Now and again one of the Egyptian Army sentries, which the conspirators in Cairo had given him for protection, would stop, cock his rifle and stand, head half-inclined to the night breeze, listening for a moment or two in tense expectancy before continuing his round.

The Count grinned. They were still fearful. They had received the radio message from Yassa an hour before and he had told them there was no further danger of pursuit. Yet the Egyptians could not rid themselves of their fears. Squatting on the hard stony ground in the way he had learned from the

Arabs so many years before, he took another sip of his precious whisky and glanced at El Nouri's cunning face.

The tiny ex-chief-of-staff, who, although he was Moslem enough to refuse the Count's offer of a drink, was nevertheless smoking a cigarette, holding it in the Turkish fashion between the little finger and the one next to it and inhaling through his clenched fist. Thus he obeyed at least the letter of the Moslem law and did not allow the tobacco to touch his lips.

Count Kun, who was a chain-smoker, lit another cheap *Afrika Korps* rationed 'V-cigarette' and stubbed out its predecessor. He took another sip of his whisky. It was a celebration of a kind, but he couldn't allow himself more than one drink this night; there was a long way to go yet.

'So, Nouri Pasha, the English are dead.'

The General shook his head. 'You trust the report?'

'*Natuerlich*. Your Lieutenant Yassa is a good man. He is a realist – something unusual in an Egyptian.'

Nouri Pasha chuckled. 'His father was a Turk like mine, you know.'

Kun grinned. His humour was occasioned by the thought that Nouri Pasha's father had been a Turk all right, but he had been a Jew too. What would the Fuehrer say if he knew that the man who was going to help the Third Reich change the whole character of the desert war was a Jew! That would shake them in Berlin.

'When I went out there in 1906 as a young soldier,' the General pointed in the direction of Libya, 'before the Italians took it off us, we used to treat the Delta Egyptians like that.' He clicked his fingers contemptuously.

The Count laughed. 'You Turks are little better than the Germans. You have all the same racial prejudices.' He sought for the Arabic word. 'You are a … superior people.'

The General stared across at the Austrian. Then he lifted his head in that typically Turkish way, moving it back swiftly: a gesture that could mean either denial or disbelief. 'Perhaps, Kun Pasha, perhaps. But what now?'

Kun felt the familiar itch and his lips started to grow dry. Soon he would have to hurry to his tent. 'We go south now, due south,' he said, with an expansive gesture of his skinny arm, scarred with the myriad marks of the needle.

'South?' Nouri echoed. He was a brave man. Ataturk himself had decorated him before the British had captured him and shipped him to Malta, and at Gallipoli he had been wounded three times, but his wrinkled face mirrored his fear. 'There is nothing out there – nothing. That leads to the heart of the desert.'

The Count laughed but said no more.

'My son once tried to find a way,' Nouri went on, 'you know what happened to him.' The sentence was left hanging in the oppressive night air, and tears welled up in the old man's eyes.

The Count's laugh died on his lips. He rose, 'Come, Nouri Pasha. It is time to sleep. Tomorrow will be long.' Kun put his arm around the old man's shoulders and guided him to his tent. Soon it would be time for the needle. 'Do not concern yourself with our route, General,' he said. 'I shall take care of it. I know the way.'

Outside the General's tent, they shook hands in the Arabic fashion, then Kun turned and limped back to his own. His limbs were beginning to tremble and the sweat was already standing out on his brow. Greedily, almost frantically, he seized the pack containing the needle. With fumbling, nail-bitten fingers he pulled back the straps.

3

'Look, sir...' Stevens began.

Crooke clamped his hard hand over the Cockney's mouth. 'Yes, I can see it,' he said softly, as the little group crouched in the narrow wadi in the pre-dawn darkness.

He whispered urgently to the guardsman. 'Peters, over here. Your eyes are better than mine. What can you make out?'

The ex-CSM took a breath and then executed the old desert trick of turning his head to one side and swinging it to the front, with his eyes held down to the ground. A moment's pause. He looked up suddenly and everything loomed up a lighter black against the black background. 'It all looks quiet, sir. I think they're all kipping... I can count three shapes to the left of the site ... and one, no, two of them sleeping to the right.'

'That's five of them accounted for then,' Crooke said. The rest of them crouched behind him expectantly. Crooke could almost feel the new loyalty and respect. His plan of the day before had visibly impressed them. Gippo had looked at him afterwards, once they had run through the gauntlet of enemy fire, as if he were some kind of clairvoyant who could read the future.

It had been a simple enough trick, however. He knew the heights would be the obvious place for an ambush; three miles off he had ordered them to place the sandbags in position, covering the top halves with their sand goggles and masks. Then he had told them to get down on the floor and had taken over the wheel himself. As soon as the firing broke out they pulled the sandbags down and used them for protection. Fortunately the enemy were poor shots, though one of the last rounds had nicked him, drawing a little blood.

Then they had waited for night to fall and leaving their truck behind in the desert, had worked their way back to the site of the ambush on the assumption that their attackers would not move camp till morning. The guardsman's keen eyes confirmed that assumption.

'What now, sir?'

'Well, we can assume from the volume of fire that there are more of them than the five we can see. My guess is that the rest will be on the top of the hill – and all asleep just like their sentries.' He indicated the general direction of the five sleeping close to the trail. 'So I'm going to leave you, Jones, to cover the sentries while the rest of us go up the back.' He nodded to the steep cliff behind them. 'Once you hear firing from up top, let them have it.'

Crooke moved off to the cliff, with the rest following him, stumbling occasionally in the darkness, trying at the same time to make as little noise as possible. All of them knew that silence was essential if they were going to surprise their unknown enemy. At the foot of the cliff, Crooke paused and looked up at the sharp black silhouette. 'It looks a tough bugger,' Stevens remarked, echoing his own unspoken thoughts.

Crooke thought for a moment. 'All right, we've got to go up singly. I think that's our best bet.' He turned and stared at the white blobs of their faces in the darkness. 'Who wants to go first?'

Surprisingly enough, it was the guardsman who volunteered. Slinging his rifle over his shoulder, he stepped forward. 'I'll have a bash, sir. I used to do a bit of scrambling up the cliffs as a lad.'

'Good man – and good luck,' Crooke whispered.

The guardsman reached up until he found a handhold and started pulling himself up. 'This looks OK,' he whispered and disappeared into the darkness. Digging his toes into the sandy rock of the cliff face and clinging till the ends of his fingers were numb with pain, he edged his way up inch by inch. In spite of the coldness of the night, the sweat began to pour off him. It soaked his clothes and almost blinded him. For six yards he crawled through murderous camel thorn that tore and ripped at his flesh. Once he hung perilously by his hands, not able to move for the thorns that had fastened themselves to his ripped shorts. Desperately, he twisted and turned to release himself from the barbs that were biting into his flesh. As one gave another lashed forward against his face, tearing the flesh in a dozen spots. He stifled a cry of agony, feeling the blood running down his face into his mouth. Behind him he could hear the rest of the party making a better go of it, following his trail, finding the way cleared of its worst obstacles at the expense of his torn and bleeding body. He put the toe of his boot in a hole in the rock and reached his hand up to the sharp edge of a flattish rock just above his head. The foothold gave. His hand slipped and the rock ripped off a fingernail, sending a wave of almost unbearable pain through his body. He swung his face into the dirt to stifle his cries.

Then he'd made it! Before him he saw the clearly defined edge of the cliff, outlined against the soft purple of the pre-dawn sky. He clawed his way over the edge and collapsed on the flat ground, the blood pouring from his lacerated face.

A few minutes later the others appeared. They flung themselves in the sand at the top of the cliff and lay there panting.

Crooke was first on his feet. With legs that were strangely rubbery, he moved away a few yards towards the direction of the enemy camp and said in a hoarse voice that he still did not have under control, 'Well done, guardsman, a good show. All right, lads, on your feet.'

They did as they were ordered, unslinging their weapons automatically. Cautiously they descended on the sleeping camp – a half-dozen small belltents – in the saucerlike depression of the cliff's top.

Now the sky was beginning to flush its first dramatic red. Everything was suddenly sharp, hard and brittle, bathed in a warm, blood-red blinding light. In ten or fifteen minutes more, the sun would be up and the ground would begin to burn. But for the moment the air was cool and clear; ideal for the slaughter which would soon commence.

'All right, lads,' Crooke said softly. 'They've got a sentry, too. Just this side of the first tent.'

'He looks as if he's kipping,' Stevens whispered, 'shall I take him.'

Crooke shook his head. He pointed to Gippo who had drawn his long knife. Gippo needed no urging. At the double, his body crouched, he ran forward. Suddenly the sentry stirred. In the clear air, the watching men could see every detail. Slowly, almost stupidly, he opened his eyes. In a moment he would see them. Gippo was ten yards away now.

Then he saw them. His face registered shocked indignation. He opened his mouth to shout, grabbing at his rifle. Gippo threw himself forward. The two fell to the ground. A knife rose in the air. The watchers saw its blade gleam in the rays of the rising sun. It flashed down. There was a wet cutting sound, a muffled scream. A moment later Gippo was on his feet, waving the blood-stained knife above his head.

'Come on,' Crooke hissed. He ran forward,

revolver clasped in his hand, the other three after him.

From one of the tents came a cry of alarm, followed by a string of frightened Arabic. A man ran naked out of the first tent, followed by another clad in a white loincloth with unlaced boots flapping on his feet. He held a rifle in his hand. Stevens raced past the murdered sentry and raised his sten. The naked man screamed and dropped to his knees, punching holes in the sand with his clenched fist, while the blood spurted from the holes in his body.

The other man dropped instinctively and raised his rifle. Sand spurted up in front of Thaelmann. He stopped. Without even seeming to take aim, he fired his rifle from the hip. The man with the unlaced boots rolled backwards, the rifle still held in his lifeless hands.

The first shots had their effect. Screaming men flooded out of the tents, weapons clutched in their hands. The attackers rushed on, firing as they came. From down below the cliff they heard the high-pitched burr, which revealed that the Yank had gone into action with his Schmeisser.

'The second tent, sir!' Gippo screamed suddenly.

Thaelmann swung round. A hail of fire tore up the sand in front of him. A plump man with sergeant's stripes on the sleeve of his khaki shirt was squatting behind an ammo box firing a bren. Thaelmann lifted his rifle and fired once. The man dropped the automatic as if it were red hot. He went head first over the ammo box, his neck doubled under him.

Dead and dying men lay everywhere. There was a sudden movement from the last tent. Stevens swung round from the hip and fired. The slugs ripped through the tent wall. Scream after scream rang from inside. But Stevens kept his finger on the trigger. Then the screams stopped. Stevens staggered back as if utterly exhausted.

The guardsman found himself alone. Suddenly a young man, lighter than the rest, loomed up in front of him, his fist clenched round a .38. The guardsman flung up his rifle instinctively. 'Drop it!' he yelled. Slowly, very slowly, it seemed almost like the slow-motion shots Peters remembered from the pre-war Pathe newsreels, the revolver came level with his stomach. The guardsman swallowed. Instinctively he lifted up his rifle. With the butt he smashed the man across his face. There was the brittle crack of a breaking jaw.

A few minutes later it was all over. The tented camp was a bloodstained shambles of dead men, scuffed sand, gleaming cartridge cases, the only sound the soft moans of the sergeant who had fired the bren. Silence descended on the scene. Softly, Crooke whispered through lips cracked and flecked a little with blood, 'Thank you, lads. You put up a good show.'

The sergeant, his wounded arm and shoulder bound up with a makeshift sling and a field-dressing sat in the sun, mumbling fearfully to himself, tears rolling unheeded down his fat dark face, as guardsman Peters passed from him to the young officer. The man's face was one livid bruise stretching from the right cheek down to the lower left jaw where the rifle butt had hit him.

Peters looked at it and clicked his tongue in what might have been regret. 'That looks nasty,' he murmured.

Yassa glared up at him from where he was slumped with his back against a ration box, his eyes full of hate. He said nothing. Peters opened another field-dressing and bent down to apply the lint to the injured man's face. Before he reached it, Yassa's hand knocked it savagely away.

Peters swallowed hard. 'I'm only trying to help,' he said and tried again. The Egyptian hawked throatily and spat straight into his face. Slowly, very slowly, Peters stood up, the spit dripping from his face. Before he had decided how to retaliate a voice behind him said cynically, 'That's what you get for trying to treat them niggers like human beings.' Jones grinned and raised the Colt he was carrying with the five fresh marks carved in the butt for the men he had killed an hour before. 'They only understand it if you treat 'em like the animals they are.' He turned his attention to the two surviving Egyptians. 'You,' he pointed the pistol at the sergeant, 'move your fat butt.'

The NCO might not have understood English, but he understood the gesture all right. He leapt to his feet as if he had been stung by a scorpion. The American grinned. He looked down at the lieutenant. 'You too, brother.'

Slowly, the lieutenant got to his feet. The American raised his foot and rammed it hard into the back of the Egyptian's leg. He howled with pain and sank to his knees. Jones reached down and, seizing Yassa by his hair, pulled him up. Ignoring the other two, he pushed his hard face close to Yassa's whose eyes were filled with tears and almost bulging from his head, and said: 'Next time I say move, buddy, you move! *Understand?*'

'For God's sake, give over,' Peters cried, hurt and shocked by the brutality of it all. 'Why the hell do you have to act so damn tough?'

The American looked at him for a moment. 'Soldier, if you'd have been raised the way I was, you'd have learned to be tough. If you didn't you didn't eat, and one morning they'd find ya stretched out in the cabin – stiff.'

'Bring them over, Jones,' Crooke's voice broke into the exchange. The American pushed them forward to where Crooke stood in the middle of the wrecked Egyptian camp. 'Gippo, come over here,' he commanded, 'I need you to interpret.'

'Yes sir,' Gippo replied smartly and left off looting the bodies sprawled around the camp. He hurried over, proudly displaying three silver rings on his right hand and a cheap metal-strapped wrist watch on each wrist. Crooke pointed to Yassa: 'Ask him who ordered them to ambush us here and where that person is now.'

Yassa took his hand away from his swollen

face and spoke for the first time, 'You don't need an interpreter,' he said in fluent, almost accentless English, 'I was at Balliol.'

'All right then, you heard the questions. Let's have an answer – *quick!*'

Yassa kept his lips firmly pressed together, a look of defiance on his swollen but still handsome young face. The others watched him curiously; at his side the fat sergeant cringed, not understanding, yet well aware of the look in the American's eyes.

'Don't be a fool, man,' Crooke rapped. 'Can't you see that you're completely expendable to those traitors back in Cairo? Do you think that they'll back you up once we take you to GHQ? Within a matter of hours, we'll have you court-martialled and they won't lift a finger to stop you being hanged. As an apparently educated young man, you shouldn't need to be told that.'

The young man shrugged. 'So, if they do hang me, there will be others who will follow me.' He licked his dry lips. 'The people of Cairo.'

Crooke looked at him in contempt. 'The people of Cairo! That mob! They'd run like rats, faced by a platoon of British infantry.' Yassa flushed angrily. 'If you kill me, there will be hundreds of others. Do you think

138

you can stop the progress of a whole nation by killing me or a hundred other patriots like me?'

Thaelmann, standing just behind Crooke, looked at the young officer with interest. An observer could easily have read the way his mind was working by the expression on his face. But no one was looking at Thaelmann; their interest was concentrated on the two officers.

'You British turn your machine guns on a crowd of unarmed natives,' Yassa said hotly. 'You mow them down and then stick up the Union Jack, saying, "this is ours". Thereafter you build a few roads, a railway or two and send a few rich men's sons to Oxford so they'll be your willing collaborators. Then you begin to loot the place. You give yourselves a mission which is a cover for twenty per cent dividends and safe markets. Nothing to do with King and Country and the civilizing mission – the rest of the mealy-mouthed claptrap...'

Suddenly Crooke leant forward and slapped him hard across the face. *That's enough,*' he shouted. 'I'm no politician, I'm a soldier and all I know is that you are going to die. And you are going to die now!' Abruptly he turned round and said to Peters, 'You take him away and shoot him, d'you understand?'

The guardsman did not move and Crooke stared at him blindly as if his mind were too worked up to grasp what was happening.

'I'll take him,' a soft voice broke the sudden tension. It was the American. He walked over to the lieutenant. 'OK,' he said quietly with none of his usual toughness, 'let's go.'

Obediently, almost tamely, the lieutenant allowed himself to be pushed forward. Together the two of them disappeared behind one of the bullet-holed tents. A moment later there was a muffled crack. Stevens licked his lips, looked at Crooke's blank face, then flashed a significant look at Gippo.

Jones reappeared, walking slowly towards them, stuffing his pistol back into his holster. He avoided looking at the little group standing in front of the Egyptian sergeant, who was sobbing softly to himself, his fat face buried in his plump unwounded hand. Five minutes later he began to talk.

4

It was nearly thirty-six hours later, driving due south, that they had proof that the wounded Egyptian sergeant, sleeping with the rest in the back of the dust-covered truck, had been speaking the truth. Thaelmann, who was driving, hit the brakes hard and nearly sent a dozing Crooke flying into the butt of the twin Lewis guns.

'What is it?' he cried, waking immediately.

Thaelmann pointed to the desert in front of them. *'Trucks,* sir... Look over there, in that wadi!'

Crooke reacted instinctively. 'Bail out,' he cried.

The crew grabbed their weapons and flung themselves over the truck's sides. Dropping into the sand they took up their defensive positions, their weapons cocked and ready for immediate action.

But nothing happened.

The little laager of trucks in the wadi lay stark and silent. No stream of tracer hissed their way. Crooke, who had flung himself under the front of the truck with Thaelmann and drawn his .38 in the same movement, let it drop. He stuffed the revolver back in its holster and took out his field glasses. He focused them and surveyed the silent vehicles carefully. Finally he lowered them and said: 'They're Chevvies too. Like our truck.'

He turned to Jones who was squatting next to Peters. 'You two, fan out to left and right and give me cover.'

'Okay, lootenant,' the American answered, unslinging his Schmeisser.

He nudged Peters in the ribs. 'All right Charlie, let's move, eh.' His voice was almost friendly, or as friendly as it could ever be. Crooke turned to Stevens. 'You get behind the Lewis guns. If anything starts, fire over our heads.' Then the three of them advanced towards the group of vehicles.

But Crooke's precautions were unnecessary. The laager was empty and had been for some time, judging by the layer of sand which covered their bonnets and hoods. He turned and waved to the rest to bring up the truck.

'What is it?' Stevens asked.

'A laager of one of the patrols, though I've never known them get this far south before.'

He pointed to the unit sign at the back of the nearest truck, to confirm his statement. 'You see,' he explained, 'they place them out on their route as a reserve. Like the Arabs did in the old days. They never ventured into the desert without second camels.'

'Like Father Xmas in the desert-middle?' Gippo quipped in his fractured English. He crossed to one of the trucks and undoing the flap pointed to the big container which lay there. 'Fifty gallon can of water, sir.'

'Oh, boy,' the American chortled with surprising enthusiasm, rubbing his stubbly chin, 'with that kind of water you could get a real bath!'

Ever since they had left the Citadel, Crooke had only allowed them a pint of water a day for washing and general ablutions. For his part he had followed the old desert ritual of washing one third of his body with the water ration every day, working from the face downwards and then at the beginning of the fourth day starting from the toes upwards again.

'And there's plenty of bully over here, sir,' Stevens cried out, standing in the back of another of the vehicles. He slung a sixteen-ounce can at Gippo. 'There you are, you thieving nignog, get yer choppers into that!'

He turned to the rest. 'There's enough bully here lads to buy fat Fatimah at the Kit-Kat and her mother too.'

Crooke let them wander through the dozen or so vehicles looting what they could find, shouting to each other like excited schoolboys when they discovered something new. He relaxed in the front of their truck and watched them with pleasure. They needed time to relax. The past few days had been hard and God knows what the next few held for them.

Abruptly he was jerked from his mood of relaxation by Thaelmann's urgent: 'Sir … sir, look at this, will you?'

Thaelmann was running excitedly across the sand with what looked like a wad of coloured paper in his hand.

'What is it?'

Thaelmann thrust it into Crooke's hand. 'Look at the first sheet,' he said breathlessly.

Crooke looked down and read the name aloud slowly, *Der Signal*... German, eh?'

'Yes, sir,' Thaelmann agreed, hardly able to contain his excitement.

'The German Forces magazine,' Crooke commented. 'I've seen it before.' Idly he looked through the wad of paper, torn into rough squares. They were mostly good quality, coloured pictures of bronzed young men in *Afrika Korps* peaked caps, lounging at the sides of Mark IV tanks or 88mm guns gazing with bored superiority at long lines of ragged British POWs in absurdly long, drooping shorts. *'Das britische Empire ... am Kreuzweg ... im nahen Osten,'* he read one of the captions slowly and translated. 'The British Empire ... at the crossroads ... in the Near East,' he paused and handed the wad back to the German, who could apparently hardly contain his excitement. 'Well, that lying little bugger Goebbels is right enough there, Thaelmann. But what's so important about it? You'll get heat stroke running around like that.'

With his innate Prussian sense of discipline, Thaelmann waited till Crooke finished. 'You see, sir, I had to go to the latrine.' He indicated a spot behind the nearest dune. 'I found an old *Donnerbalken* – a thunder box, as you call it – a couple of ration boxes with a pole nailed between them to sit on.'

'Yes, I know,' Crooke interrupted. 'Get on with it, man.' Like most Germans, Thaelmann was exceedingly long-winded when he got started, which was not often, fortunately.

'Well, sir, there was no Army Form Blank. Just this,' he held up the wad of paper.

'All right, so you found the *Signal* there. So what?'

'But look at this date, sir,' Thaelmann said. He thrust the first page of the wad under Crooke's nose.

Crooke read the date aloud in a slow voice. *'The twenty-fifth of August 1942!'*

'The day we left the Citadel,' Thaelmann said softly, realizing he had got his point across as he stared at an open-mouthed Crooke.

'And how would a German Army magazine find its way here by this time, sir, unless...' He left the question unfinished.

'So Kun was here before us,' Crooke said softly. They had cleaned up everything before they left, but they forgot the latrine. It was apart from the laager – an easy place to overlook. 'Gippo and Stevens,' Crooke shouted at the two inveterate looters, working their way swiftly from truck to truck.

The scavengers paused in their attempts to break open a compo ration box.

'Check the petrol truck – the one over there. See if the drums are still full.'

A few moments later the answer came

146

back. 'Bone dry, sir.'

'Thank you,' he said and dropping from the cab of their own truck, he walked over to the nearest one in the laager, followed by Thaelmann. He opened the cap of the nearest petrol tank and taking off his revolver lanyard, dangled it inside the container. When he brought it out again, there was no sign of discoloration. 'Not a drop,' he muttered.

Together they passed on to the next one and the next. All the tanks were empty. The whole laager was without petrol. He paused and looked at Thaelmann. 'They could afford to leave the water and the food. They obviously had plenty of that. But petrol is always a problem. Now we know we're getting close to them.'

He called over to Gippo and Stevens again. 'All right, you two, get the Egyptian to help you to rustle up the food. Double water rations for the lot and break out as much M & V as you like.' He bent over the front of their own truck and pulled out a bottle wrapped in a towel. He handed it over to Stevens, whose face beamed with pleasurable surprise when he removed the towel. 'Johnny Walker,' he breathed, looking at its tattered label.

'Yes, break it out among the men tonight after char. They deserve it. And tell them that we're making an early start tomorrow, two hours before dawn.'

Crooke scratched his head in bewilderment. Everything seemed to be running to plan. But one thing puzzled him. If Kun had set off from Cairo on the same day as they had, or perhaps even a few hours earlier, how did he come to possess a paper dated 25th August 1942?

5

It was furnace hot and above them the sky was the colour of wood smoke. No wind stirred. As the Chevvy bumped its way across the burning sand, zig-zagging round the huge boulders which littered the route, Crooke shaded his eyes and stared up at the sky. The sun was like a coin seen dimly at the bottom of a dirty pool. He shuddered a little for he knew the signs.

Trying to take his mind off what might soon come, he tapped the guardsman on the shoulder. 'All right, Peters, we can park here. Let's have a bit of a break.'

Gratefully, Peters pulled up and sat for a moment, not moving, the sweat running unheeded down his brown face. Slowly the others bestirred themselves and clambered over the side of the truck. A couple went to urinate, but the exercise was painful. Their kidneys had suffered too much these past eight hours. The rest crouched with their backs against the side of the truck, all spirit knocked out of them by the hellish journey across the sand.

Crooke rose stiffly and dropped to the ground. He stared at his exhausted crew for a moment. Their shirts were already bleached a dirty yellow and their new boots were beginning to turn white. Their faces were leaner, lips drawn fine, eyes keen and reddened by the sand particles. They looked typical veterans of the desert, as if they had been 'up the blue' for years.

He licked his lips and said, 'I reckon we can't be far behind them now.'

There was no response. Even the American seemed to have lost his usual lust for combat. But their lack of enthusiasm did not worry him. They were tired but still a highly individualistic body of men who could be depended upon to fight to the end if called on to do so. They had nothing to lose anyway. None of them so far as he could gather, had any dependants, any possessions – nothing save what they stood up in. They were his completely, cut off from yesterday, living for today, their only hope tomorrow.

'When we catch up with them, let's get the drill straight. Avoid gunplay if you can. I want this Kun and the General alive if possible. But if they cause trouble, don't hesitate, shoot the first man who makes a hostile move or any other kind of move. Because he'll have recovered from the shock of seeing you with a gun. He has then started to think and therefore he's dangerous.' He licked his dry lips, but before he could continue, the American said:

'And then you plug the guy next to you. He's the best placed to give you a bad time, see.' He clicked his forefinger like pulling the trigger of a gun. 'The rest is up to you.'

In spite of his weariness, Crooke smiled slightly. They were all seasoned professionals; they needed no fancy briefing. But how would they react to what was going to happen soon? They would be facing up to something which was more destructive than any barrage of 88mms. Anxiously he looked at the sky. He remembered the old Arab saying: 'Death is a black camel which knocks at every man's door.' Soon that black camel would come knocking at their door, that he knew.

The sandstorm caught them an hour later. The sun vanished abruptly. A gust of wind hit the truck with such force that it was stopped dead.

'All right,' Crooke yelled above the roar. 'This is it!' He had been expecting the storm for hours but he had refused to take cover until it was on them; he had wanted to keep close to their quarry.

'For God's sake don't let yourselves be blown over the side! If you do, wedge yourselves under the wheels.' He cupped his hand around his mouth to be heard above the ever-increasing bedlam of sound. 'Hang on with all you've got... Once it starts blowing you across the desert – you're a goner!'

He dropped among the men crouched in the back of the Chevvy, grabbing hold of the Lewis guns with both hands.

Then it was on them in full force.

At a hundred miles an hour the wind hit them like a wall of hot stilettos, striking at their naked faces with lethal ferocity. Sand particles hissed through their thin clothing. They opened their mouths to howl with pain, but the wind snatched the words from their mouths.

Breathing became difficult. The howling, hellish fog of sand snatched the air from their lungs and they coughed like old, asthmatic men. Above their heads the ululating threnody rose to an ever louder pitch. It had travelled a thousand miles across the desert to seize them and it was not to be denied its victims. Time and time again it battered them with a gigantic fist. Once, in a momentary pause, Crooke forced his head up and peered through his sand-caked goggles. For a fleeting second he thought he saw something dark outlined against the lighter sand wall. But it was more imagined than seen and the next moment the wind was on them again. He ducked his head fearfully. With renewed force the wind shrieked and wailed furiously across the desert, as if some god on high had ordained that these puny mortals should be wiped from the face of the earth because of their temerity in penetrating his burning kingdom.

Then, as suddenly as it had begun, it was

over. The maddening howl was replaced by a soft, ever-decreasing dirge. Then it was gone altogether and silence filled the desert. For a while the sand-covered men in the back of the truck did not move, as if they did not dare believe the ordeal was over.

Blindly, with arms outstretched like sightless men, they reached forward to feel their bodies. For that was what they were: blind men. Crooke put out a hand. The sand dropped heavily from it. He felt for his goggles and rubbed them clear. Next to him he saw what he took to be the guardsman in the driving seat. The entire front of his body was solidly encrusted in a gleaming layer of bright new sand. Crooke ran his tongue round his lips. A thick wet streak broke the mask that covered the lower half of his face. He pulled off his goggles and stared out at the transformed desert. Its surface was utterly changed by the sandstorm.

'Yer like the original chocolate-coloured coon himself,' a voice said, spitting out particles of sand at the same time. It was Stevens, staring at Gippo, whose eyes were surrounded by two huge sand-free circles where he had removed his goggles.

'Are we all accounted for?' Crooke asked.

'Where's the Kraut?' the American asked,

spitting sand.

'I'm here,' a voice came from below, followed by a curse in German. *'Verdammte Scheisse!'*

Crooke looked over the side.

The German was wedged between the wheel and a huge boulder that had been blown against the truck during the storm. The wind had drowned its impact. 'I can't get out,' Thaelmann cried.

'You sure do look dinky down there, tucked away in your little bed,' the American cracked.

'Break out the spades,' Crooke ordered and jumped out of the truck to see what other damage the wind had inflicted. Obediently the rest grabbed the spades and set about freeing the helpless German.

Five minutes later, when they had freed Thaelmann, Crooke asked, 'Where's the Egyptian?' They paused in the midst of their labour, the sweat pouring from their foreheads with the effort.

'Yes, where's the wog?' Gippo queried.

But another and strange voice answered their question for them.

'You will kindly put your hands up,' a soft, pleasant foreign voice commanded, 'otherwise we must fire.'

They spun round. As he turned, Crooke, a little slower than the rest, realized he had been right about the dark object he had thought he saw during the storm. With a sinking feeling he knew what he would see behind him.

A line of perhaps twenty or more Egyptian soldiers stood facing them on the crest of one of the new sand dunes, rifles levelled threateningly. A little way in front there was the escaped sergeant, a revolver in his good hand. And next to him stood a tall, emaciated European of about forty-five, armed with a machine pistol. It had been the European who had given the command.

Now he spoke again. 'Carefully, but very carefully please – will you lower your hands – those of you who are armed – and release your weapons.' Warily he watched while Crooke and the American undid their holsters and dropped them softly into the sand.

'Now raise them again.'

They did as they were ordered.

The European was satisfied. Slowly he came toward them, his long head to one side, his eyes filled with pain like a dentist advancing on a frightened child, the forceps hidden by the side of his apron and fearful of hurting it. He walked with a pronounced limp.

He stopped when he was a dozen yards away. Crooke could see every detail of his raddled face with its yellow unhealthy colour and tortured eyes. He bowed slightly with Central European formality like some ancient professor.

'May I introduce myself, Lieutenant Crooke?' he said in his soft, slightly accented voice. 'My name is Kun – Graf Kun vom Regiment Brandenburg.'

6

For a long time now the strange-looking German from Admiral Canaris's élite spy and sabotage regiment had been discussing them with the little Egyptian General, whom they had come so far to find. The two of them, crouched around the burning petrol stove, spoke fluent Arabic and, at a distance of twenty yards or so, it was difficult for Crooke to follow their conversation. But El Nouri's vicious 'kill them', repeated at least a dozen times with harsh vehemence told

156

Crooke all he wanted to know about their discussions.

But the Count did not seem to agree with the Egyptian's decision. He seemed to be pleading with the other man. Crooke could not understand why he should plead for their lives. By now he must surely know about the trap they had sprung on Lieutenant Yassa and his men and how they had executed that officer in cold blood. No doubt the wounded sergeant, happy and boastful after his successful escape during the sandstorm, must have related every detail of what had happened on the top of the cliff. He wasn't the type to escape an opportunity like that. He looked across to where the fat NCO sat among a crowd of soldiers, his neck adorned with one of the strange silk-like scarves they all wore – obviously he shared the typical Egyptian's delight in silk – gesticulating excitedly as he told them his story.

He sat back among his silent fellow prisoners, who had now sunk into a fitful sleep, seeking the only way out of their despair at being captured after all they had gone through to catch up with El Nouri. He recalled Mallory's face as they had parted at the Citadel. Mallory was clever, but flippant, not fully realizing what the war was about. But at that moment in the Citadel Crooke knew that Mallory understood the vital importance of their mission; that if they did not recapture the Egyptian chief-of-staff, it could well mean the end of the Desert War.

The discussions around the fire had ended. El Nouri was walking away to his tent leaving the Austrian sitting staring into the flickering blue flame of the petrol fire, pulling at one of the evil, black-tobacco German cigarettes which he smoked continually.

The Austrian had treated them well in the past few hours. They had had all the water they wanted as well as a handful of dates and a slice of tinned pumpernickel bread, the first bread they had tasted since they had entered the desert. When they had stopped an hour or so before to make camp for the night and the Egyptian sergeant, egged on by his jeering companions, had started to taunt the American, the Count had stepped in and quickly put an end to the suddenly threatening situation. What was going on in the man's mind?

A few minutes later he found out. Kun rose from the fire and limped painfully towards him. He looked down at Crooke.

He caught the British officer's quick glance at his leather belt and smiled faintly like a fond parent noting the first signs of intelligence in his child. 'No, my dear Crooke, I am not armed. It would not be worth attempting to seize me. Besides,' he nodded to two armed sentries a dozen yards away, 'what could you do against them, eh?'

Crooke did not answer.

Carefully the German knelt down at his side and spoke softly, as if he was worried about waking the sleeping men. 'The old man,' he indicated the General's tent, 'wants to have you killed. He is a typical Turk – in my early days they called them the Prussians of the Near East for good reason – he sees things solely in blacks and whites. I do not want to kill you, however. For the past half hour, as you have undoubtedly been aware, we have been arguing for your lives. I won. And I want to give you a chance.'

'Why?' Crooke asked. 'We didn't give that young lieutenant a chance, did we?'

'Because, my dear Crooke, you and I are alike. If it had not been for this terrible war, we could have been friends.'

'How do you mean?'

'I have heard of you, Crooke. In Berlin we

have a small file on you. We've had it ever since the Rommel business. Canaris is a wise old man, even if he surrounds himself with people who will one day bring him to the executioner's axe. But no matter. People like you, we feel, are sometimes more dangerous than a whole battalion of trained fighting troops. But that is not my reason for feeling … er *sympathetisch* – what a lack that in English you have no similar word in your vocabulary – towards you.' He paused and stared out over the darkening desert as if he expected to see something.

'No, it is not that. You are a man like I am: a man who loves the desert, you have a feel for it. When we are here, we hate its discomfort, its filthy heat, its danger, but once we are back in so-called civilization…' he shrugged his thin shoulders eloquently.

Crooke looked at him and realized that the man was sincere.

'I shall not tell you too much, Crooke, for that would be revealing secrets, those stupid military secrets of theirs. But when I joined Canaris four years ago, it was specifically for the purpose of coming back to *my* desert.'

For a moment Crooke was tempted to ask what had happened to the Youngblood expedition and how Kun had managed to survive it, but some sixth sense warned him not to.

The German held out his hand. It contained a compass. 'Take it,' he said, and taking out his note book scribbled a few figures on it. He ripped off the sheet and passed it to Crooke. 'A compass bearing,' he explained, 'to the El Kharga Oasis which is about a hundred and fifty miles due north-east of here.'

'But what is all this?' Crooke asked, staring at the other man's face in complete bewilderment.

'Because at dawn I'm going to allow you and your men to go free. You, *mein lieber* Crooke, must also survive this terrible conflict and perhaps in better times, we shall meet again under different and happier circumstances.' He paused, and his face creased in a worried frown. 'But all I shall allow you in the way of water is four bottles each – perhaps eight litres.'

Crooke did a quick sum in his head. 'That's only about a quart a day if we could make El Kharga in a week,' he protested.

'Yes, I know. It was the old man who made that his final condition for your release. As you could see he gave in reluctantly, but like most of his kind he had to have the last word.' He hesitated, as if he wondered whether he should say the next words. 'That water ration appeals to his mentality, you know... His last words to me before he went to his tent were, *"So you want them to live. I don't. In this way both of us will come to our rights... I hope, for my part, that the whole cursed lot of them will die a slow death – a very slow death in the desert".'*

The Count's convoy moved out at four the next morning. Their parting had been cool and correct. There were none of the confidences of the previous evening. The Egyptian sergeant, had filled their water bottles with careless generosity, spilling great quantities of the precious fluid on the sand as if to torment them in advance. Now the trucks were starting to pull away, stark black against the horizon.

In silence the six men watched them go. In spite of the cool dawn, none of them moved. They seemed frozen to the spot, as if for eternity, their eyes fixed greedily on the departing trucks, which moved steadily farther away. Finally when they were just black spots against the red glow, the spell was broken.

Crooke seemed unmoved by their terrible

predicament. He cleared his throat and said, 'Pay attention to me. I'll not fool you, we're in a fix. Now there are two courses open to us. We can go like the Count said to the El Kharga Oasis some one hundred and fifty miles from here.'

'And the other?'

'We can follow them.'

'*What?*' the American said.

'We can follow them,' Crooke repeated drily without any apparent emotion.

'But no one has ever been going that way, sir,' Gippo protested. 'I am well informed on these things. The desert–'

'Yeah and what about their trucks?' Jones intervened. 'They'll be miles ahead of us, and what if we did catch up with them? They're armed we aren't.'

Crooke lifted up his hand to still their protests. 'I know, I know. But doesn't the fact that the Count is going on indicate that he's confident there is something out there – the other backdoor to Libya – and that backdoor can't be too far off.'

'How do you know, sir?'

'Because of the way they were handing out the water last night. You all saw how that fat Gippo NCO played around with the water when he was filling our bottles this morning.

The Count was watching him. He could have stopped him wasting the water if he had wanted to. Did you notice too that although the NCO is wounded in the shoulder, he managed to lift and tilt the water container without too much difficulty? My guess was there wasn't much more than a day's water supply left in there for the lot of them.'

'So what?' the American said. 'Perhaps they've got another laager buried out there somewhere – like your buddies of the LRDG.'

'I doubt it. I don't think El Nouri is in a fit shape to do another two thousand miles across the desert to the nearest enemy base, water or no water. You saw the shape he was in last night.'

'Well, what *are* they gonna do, Lootenant?' the American persisted.

'If only I knew,' Crooke sighed. 'One thing I do know is that they're not going to make too much progress over that–' he pointed at the boulder-littered terrain in front of them. 'I guess they won't make more than seven or eight miles an hour over that country. We could make half that mileage on foot.'

'As long as our strength held out. And that wouldn't be long,' Stevens said gloomily.

'Agreed, but assuming they'll take the

usual breaks and stop for the same period of time tonight, we *could* catch up with them in about forty-eight hours, if we kept on during the night when they're sleeping. After all the night is the best time for marching through this stuff.'

'But we still have no weapons. What'll we do if we do catch up with them?'

Crooke shrugged. 'I'll worry about that one when we get there.'

Thaelmann now broke into the discussion. 'I think we'll catch up with them a little earlier than that, sir,' he said with a queer little smile.

'Why?'

The German lifted up his sand-whitened boot. Beneath the instep was stuck a piece of plaster of the kind the Eighth Army used for desert boils. He loosened it with his nail and revealed a razor-blade. 'Those of us who escaped from the concentration camp and stayed behind in Germany swore that they would never get us in there again.' He made a gesture of slashing the blade across his wrists. 'Last night I used the blade on their tyres while you all slept.'

The American slapped Thaelmann on the back. 'For a Kraut, you're not a bad guy,' he said.

'Do you think you did a good job?' Crooke asked.

The German nodded. Without any attempt at traditional English modesty, he said: 'Yes, I did a good job. I think after a day in that,' and he pointed to the first line of boulders, 'at least three of them will have completely flat tyres.'

Crooke turned to them again: 'Well lads,' he asked, 'shall we give it a go?'

Now the response was unanimous.

The going was murderous and the temperature well over 100°. They had been going for eight hours. Three hours before the soft sand had given to hard sand again and they had lost the convoy's track. Now they were following the Count's envoy on the original compass bearing Crooke had taken just before the trucks disappeared over the horizon at dawn.

It was just as the sun began to sink that they staggered up to an abandoned truck.

'They've taken the spare.' Exhausted as he was, Stevens could not refrain from scrounging around in the hope that he would find something worth stealing. Unsteadily he pointed to where a dark circle free of sand indicated that the tyre usually fixed to the bonnet of the truck had been removed.

Crooke nodded and wiped the sweat from his forehead. He said a silent prayer of gratitude. Thank God, they were on the right track!

Carefully he bent down and felt the exhaust. Although the truck's rear was in the shade of a huge boulder, the pipe was still warm. It was clear that the Count had abandoned it only a few hours before. They weren't too far behind. 'All right,' he said, 'let's take an hour's break.'

The men needed no urging. They fell into the shade offered by the boulders all around. Peters was about to raise his waterbottle to his cracked lips, but Crooke stopped him. 'Save it,' he said, trying to speak as little as possible. 'Find a tin … we'll run the radiator water off … drink it when it's cool… Save ours.'

While the rest stared numbly at him, the guardsman drew off the water into a five galleon drum he had found at the back of the truck. Not only was it rust-coloured, it was also filled with little bits of rusted metal. But it was water and there was about a gallon and a half of it. Then they all fell into an exhausted sleep.

It was nearly dusk when Crooke went

from man to man rousing them, handing them a tin of water in turn like a mother feeding a child, saying to each of them: 'It's horrible, but it's water.'

They drank greedily and each pulled a face once their thirst had been quenched and they started to savour its rusty, oily taste.

'Get a pebble now,' he told them, 'and start sucking it. It'll get your saliva working.' The sleep in the shade and the pint and a half of rusty water had their effect. The air had begun to get cooler too and, although the sand flies started to pester them, as they always did in the period between dusk and darkness, Crooke could see that they were in better shape. 'Listen,' he said, 'they'll soon be bedding down for the night. I reckon we must be about three hours behind them now – maybe four. But if we keep it up, we might be lucky enough to catch up with them tonight.'

Slowly and stiffly they got themselves ready for the long night march. Then the whispering of the desert, starting to cool off as the sun went down, was broken by the sound of a motor – the steady drone of an aeroplane motor.

Stevens was first to react. 'Over there – a plane!'

'Quick, get down among the rocks again,' Crooke commanded.

They did not need telling twice. They threw themselves down again with surprising energy. 'Just keep your faces down,' Crooke snapped. 'They'll see the white. They're getting closer.'

The sound of the motor increased. It indicated some kind of light plane. Crooke, who was crouched behind the wrecked truck, reached up and stuck his hand on the greasy spot underneath the sump. The warm oil trickled down his palm. Hastily he smeared the stuff across his face and peered out, hoping he could see without being seen.

It was a monoplane, with a radial motor and a large cabin. And it was obviously looking for something: the motor seemed – even to his untrained ear – to be running only just above stalling speed. Every now and again it coughed alarmingly.

Slowly the plane got closer and lower until it was almost over them and Crooke ducked hastily. The engine coughed as if the pilot had suddenly taken his hand off the throttle. He had spotted the truck.

'Freeze,' Crooke cried. 'Nobody move!'

A red flare burst with a soft plop directly above them and hung blood-red in the evening sky. Slowly, very slowly, the flare began to descend to the ground until with a soft hiss, it extinguished itself in the sand.

'Don't move,' Crooke yelled. 'Let 'em move off!'

The men stayed frozen while the search plane rose and flew off to the south. Only when the plane's motor had become a faint chatter on the horizon did they crawl out of their hiding places and crowd round their black-faced commander. 'What did you make of that, sir?'

Crooke grabbed a handful of cotton waste from the back of the abandoned truck and rubbed the oil off his face. While he did so, the American answered the question for him. 'Buddy, ya don't need to spell it out. That plane was looking for somebody and it wasn't for your ugly mugs.'

'The Count?'

'Sure.'

Crooke nodded his head in agreement. 'Did anyone recognize the plane?'

It was left to Thaelmann to speak, 'Yes, it was a Fieseler Storch.'

'Yes,' Crooke agreed, 'and does anyone know the range of the Fieseler Storch?'

He answered his own question. 'Its range is about one hundred and fifty miles, one way, and the nearest German base, so far as we know, is exactly two thousand miles away.'

7

That night they sought the Count's convoy in vain. When dawn came Crooke realized to his horror that he had lost the track. As they stumbled on through the ever increasing heat of a new day, he knew that the search plane should have told him that the Count had changed his compass bearing: it had been looking for the Count's convoy too.

But he kept his knowledge to himself, although a little voice inside him whispered that he was leading his men to certain death. Yet his reason told him there was still hope. The little pieces of the mosaic of mystery surrounding the Count's destination were beginning to fall into place: the almost new copy of *Der Signal* found a thousand miles deep in the desert, the silk scarves that all the Egyptians had taken such pride in wearing, even their erstwhile prisoner, the fat Gippo sergeant, and above all, the appearance the night before of the Storch.

Just after the sun had reached its zenith the weary pursuers thought they had caught up with their quarry once more. At Crooke's command they dropped into the hot sand and stared at the little group of sandblown vehicles drawn up haphazardly in a wadi a mile away.

Their tiredness suddenly vanished, they approached cautiously, reassuring themselves that the Gippos would have to be in their tents in this heat, enjoying a siesta. This explained the convoy's uncanny silence. But as they crept closer to the vehicles, they saw there was something different about them and it became obvious that there was no sentry posted, sleeping or otherwise. In the end they gave up their attempts at concealment and openly approached the trucks.

'They're not the Gippos' trucks, sir,' Stevens said as they drew closer.

Crooke did not answer. He was as puzzled as the rest of them.

It was Peters who first identified the mysterious vehicles when they were still about a hundred and fifty yards away from the little convoy.

'They're the old Bedford fifteen hundredweights,' he exclaimed. 'Haven't seen one of them since '38.'

As they came level with the trucks, Crooke saw that he was right. They weren't even military vehicles – three ugly-snouted trucks, with old-fashioned sand tyres, buried up to their axles ... as if they had not been driven for years. Their paintwork was bleached pure white by the sun, their hoods covered in deep loads of sand. 'What do you make of it, sir?' Stevens asked.

Crooke shook his head. 'I don't rightly know.'

He seized the door of the first truck's cab. With a creak, it came off in his hand and fell to the ground. Inside a yellowed newspaper lay on the bench seat next to the wheel, as if the driver had just laid it down and gone off on some business. He twisted his neck to read the name – *The Cairo Daily Mail* – one of the capital's half-dozen English language papers. He attempted to pick it up. It crumbled up in his grasp, but not before he had caught the date – 23 June 1937.

Gippo, looking in over his shoulder, rolled his dark eyes in fear. 'This is bad – bad business, sir,' he quavered. He shook himself, as if he were suddenly cold.

Crooke pulled his head out of the cab. He

had spotted something on the back of the truck in front – faint white lettering not altogether obliterated by the ravages of time. He rubbed away some of the sand and tried to decipher the lettering. It was difficult, but once he had made out the 'Egypt' and 'Sur', he knew he had it. Slowly he read it aloud: 'The Anglo-Egyptian ... Survey ... 1937.'

'Christ on a crutch,' the American breathed in awe. 'You mean these autos have been out here since 1937 – five years?'

Crooke nodded. 'The air and the sand preserve things, you know. When I was with the LRDG we once found an armoured car patrol way out in the desert. The two cars were worthy of a museum. They dated back to 1916. Apparently they'd run out of water and died out there. They were so well preserved that we were able to start the engine of one of them.'

'Go on, sir,' Stevens said with surprising interest. 'But what about this lot?'

'Well, we've found the 1937 survey led by Colonel Youngblood, El Nouri and the Count, which ended in such a mysterious way, as I explained to you in the Citadel.'

'But what happened to them?' the guardsman asked. 'Where are the bodies?'

Five minutes later they found out. A matter of fifty yards away from the three trucks, they discovered two skeletons, half-buried by sand, their sun-bleached bones covered here and there by pieces of white rag. Peters bent down and carefully removed the sand and, sitting on his heels, indicated the farther of the two skeletons.

'That'll be Colonel Youngblood,' he said, 'he was six foot two.' He indicated the other skeleton. 'That one couldn't have been more than five five.'

Crooke agreed. 'Yes the smaller one is that of El Nouri's son, I'd guess. But how did you know?'

'Colonel Youngblood was my company commander when I first joined the Coldstream, the best company commander I ever had. We went out to India with–'

He never finished.

'Look at that hole!' It was the American. He pointed to the hole at the back of the smaller skeleton's skull. 'Someone did a pretty damn good job on him!'

'What do you mean?'

'Hell, it's obvious, ain't it? He's been shot in the back of the head. And the other one too. Look.'

There was a similar hole through the back

175

of Colonel Youngblood's skull!

So that was what had happened? Crooke glanced behind him at the three trucks. Obviously the leaders had taken a truck each when they left the rest of the survey behind. In case anything happened to one truck, or even two, they would have one to get them back. When the survivors returned, they said the leaders had been heading south with Youngblood and El Nouri Pasha's son quarrelling badly. Now the trucks were pointing due north. Clearly they were retracing their tracks. For some reason they had stopped here and the result had been murder. Murder it must have been, for there was no trace of a weapon in their hands or close by – and the only possible murder suspect had to be the Count.

Crooke bit his lip. *'But why?'* he said aloud.

The others stared at him curiously.

'And where had they been?'

But there was no answer to his questions save for the low moan of the desert wind.

It was Stevens who had the bright idea while they were hungrily munching the sloppy mess of bully beef, which they had discovered in the back of one of the trucks. The years of burning heat had reduced it to the consistency of stewed meat, which ran out through their dirty fingers. But they ate it greedily, grateful for its nourishment. Gippo was just opening another tin when Stevens paused in the middle of a mouthful and said thickly, 'You know we've had it like, sir.' He wiped his greasy hand across the front of his sun-faded shirt. 'We might even catch up with them tonight. But by that time we'd be dead beat. They could collar us like a gang of schoolkids and this time they wouldn't let us go so easily, you'd better believe that.'

Crooke didn't speak. He knew Stevens was right; he was echoing his own thoughts exactly.

'But there is one way we might get out of the shit,' he continued.

'How?'

'If you'd care to come with me, sir, I'll show you.'

Stiffly Crooke rose and followed him to where one of the trucks' bonnets was flung back. Before Crooke could stop him, Stevens had unscrewed the cap of his German water bottle and poured all the precious fluid into the radiator.

'What the devil are you up to!' Crooke yelled and knocked the Cockney's arm up.

But it was too late. The bottle was empty. Surprisingly, Stevens grinned – a painful process with his swollen sun-cracked lips.

'Not to worry, sir,' he said. 'While Gippo was scrounging around for the bully, I had a dekko at the trucks' engines. Them other two were a dead loss. But I got a spark from this one.'

'You did what?'

'I got a spark,' Stevens repeated. 'And there's more, sir. The petrol tank is half full. The sun had evaporated all the juice in the other two. But the tank on this one was in the shade of that boulder.' He pointed a grease-stained finger in the direction of the outside petrol tank. 'And there's enough oil in the sump so that the engine won't seize up straightaway at least. So if everyone of us sacrificed a pint of water each to fill up the radiator, we might get her started.'

'Started!'

'Yes, sir. In this climate she should fire easy, even if the battery's almost as dead as a doornail.' He turned and pointed to the slope that stretched up in front of them for fifty yards. 'If we could get the bitch up there, there's a downhill run on the other side of about two hundred feet before the desert levels out again. I've had a look. It'll be touch and go all right. But, God willing, we might do it!'

Stevens's plan put new heart into the almost exhausted men. Even the American gave up a pint of his precious water without a murmur of protest. The radiator filled up. Then they set to work to dig out the half-buried truck, taking turns to use the two shovels they had found, while the rest scooped away the sand with their bare hands. Half-an-hour later they were lathered in sweat and breathing harshly in the terrible heat. But the truck was free. Crooke wiped away the sweat which dripped from his eyebrows as from a leaky tap and turned to Stevens.

'All right, Y-track,' he panted, 'it's your idea. You get in and drive it.'

Stevens needed no urging. He slid behind the wheel and yelped when it touched his hands. He seized the big handbrake. For a moment it refused to move. But he gave it a kick with his boot and tried again. This time it shifted. 'All right,' he yelled cheerfully, but Crooke could see the tension in his face. He knew, as they all did, that this was their last chance. 'You can let the bitch go!'

They took the strain. The wheels gave a rusty squeak. Nothing happened. 'Once again,' Crooke yelled. They bent and heaved. 'Again!' he shouted. With all their strength they pressed their shoulders to the truck. It creaked – and then it was moving. The back-panel cracked under the thrust of Thaelmann's powerful shoulder. The wood was rotten right through.

'Scheissding!' Thaelmann cursed as he stumbled and almost fell. He caught himself in time and kept on pushing. It was vital not to let the truck stop now.

They pushed on. Their breath came in great gasps, as they toiled up the incline in the murderous sun. Crooke felt the veins at his temples hammering madly as if they were attempting to break their way out of their bone cage. Behind him the American was cursing and panting furiously. Gippo slipped and almost lost his grip. Desperately he grabbed at a stanchion. He screamed as it tore his fingers. But he did not let go. And then finally, after an eternity of pushing, panting and cursing they had it on the top of the incline, while Stevens stared down at them as they lay flat on their faces in the sand exhausted, gulping for air like a school of stranded whales.

He gave them five minutes. 'All right,' he ordered, 'you can get up now and start all over again.'

There were protests and groans, but one by one they forced themselves to their feet, standing there swaying from side to side like drunken men. Crooke swayed with them, seeing nothing save the shimmering heat waves which threatened to drown him at any moment.

'Spread yourselves out again,' Stevens ordered, completely in charge of the situation now. He looked at their sweat-lathered faces, their eyes round and unseeing, their mouths open stupidly.

'Now then gentlemen, as the immoral bawd says, once more into the breach ... let's give it one more go.' They lined up behind the vehicle.

Crooke pulled himself together. 'All right,' he said, his tongue feeling three times its normal size, 'let's get on with it.'

Stevens crashed home the gear which had not been moved for over five years. It engaged second gear. Slowly the truck breasted the incline. It began to lumber forward, gathering speed at every yard. They broke into a clumsy run. One by one they lost contact, falling flat on their faces in the sand, staring after it. Now Stevens was on his own. Still he had not lifted his foot from the clutch. A boulder loomed up in front of him! Had he seen it? *'For Chrissake,'* the American screamed, *'Look out!'*

At the very last moment, Stevens flung the wheel to one side and missed the boulder by a hair's breadth. He rumbled on. He had covered half the stretch now. Crooke found himself forcing his nails into the palm of his hand with tension. 'Come on, Y-track!' he cried, *'Come on you bastard!'*

Suddenly the truck heaved violently. A black cloud emerged from the exhaust. Crooke stopped breathing. The motor didn't start. His face sagged in despair. At his side, the American kneeling in the sand, drew his head back abruptly and cursed. The truck was gathering speed again. There were about fifty feet of slope left. Crooke let his head sink. Stevens could not possibly make it now.

Suddenly there was a long low groan, like some eerie Highland bagpipe dirge. Crooke's head flashed up. A stream of black smoke was pouring from the exhaust. The noise grew in intensity. It sounded as if the truck were going to blow up at any moment. There was a series of sharp bursts of backfire. Only thirty feet left now. A burst of white smoke, followed by violent sparks. And then there was a tremendous engine roar. The truck shot forward. A moment later it was on the flat and Stevens was gunning the engine desperately, trying to keep it going.

Crying madly, waving their arms like crazy men, their exhaustion completely forgotten, they ran down the steep slope to where a sweating, black-faced Stevens was waiting for them, gunning the engine still and grinning like a bloody fool. But Crooke was not yet quite ready to leave and the others waited while he and Peters went back to retrieve the grisly evidence of Count Kun's treachery.

The ancient truck stood up well, in spite of a few anxious moments when it gave tremendous shudders like an old and very weary animal about to give up the ghost and die. But it covered the terrain well enough at ten mph while Crooke kept an anxious eye on the country ahead and the petrol gauge's flickering red needle. In this manner they kept going for two hours. Slowly, however, Crooke began to forget the truck and its diminishing supply of fuel and concentrate more on the horizon. The character of the country began to change. Now the sand was broken up by scrubby patches of camel

183

thorn and what looked like grass. A few miles later he noted it was *definitely* grass: poor yellow parched stuff, but grass all the same. The soft wind blowing across the sand was somehow cooler too. Behind him the men shook themselves out of their lethargy under its influence and started to stare at the forbidding, completely flat-topped range of hills before them that reached up to perhaps thirteen hundred feet or more.

In silence Crooke stared with them with a feeling of disbelief. Would he wake up in a moment? Did that great red sandstone cliff really exist? Had they finally come to the end of the long search? Did the answer to the mystery lie up there on the silent plateau, which surveyed the whole desert?

Two hours later the truck gave up. She started to buck and backfire. Stevens tried to coax her on. More jerks. He changed down to second. They rolled on smoothly for a few more yards. He shoved her into neutral and thus it was that they rolled into the palms of the oasis, bathed a dull red in the reflected light of the sandstone cliff, which acted like a mirror to the sun's rays, transforming them into its own colour, and swamping everything in its own ruddy hue.

'Welcome to the Red Oasis, tourist

attraction and honeymooners' favourite,' Stevens quipped as they rolled to a stop in front of the tree-encircled bubbling spring. 'All off who wants to see the Sheik of Araby!'

They had reached the cover of the palms just in time. From above them on the top of the cliff came the roar of aeroplane engines. The next moment the little Fieseler Storch came swooping over its edge. Sharply it dropped a hundred – perhaps a hundred and fifty feet. Then the pilot caught it. The engine noise increased. The plane started to rise steeply, its cockpit glinting in the setting sun. Steadily it began to wing its way along the line of hills.

A lot of things began to fall into place in Crooke's mind.

THREE: THE BATTLE OF THE RED OASIS

'Fame – national pride – public honours –
that was all they had in their little minds!'
Count Kun to 2/Lt Crooke

1

They crouched, shivering but happy, at the foot of the cliff, now cloaked in darkness. Sitting in a circle around Crooke they nibbled the tiny, sweet dates from the palms and went on drinking the cool water, although their stomachs were distended with the amount they had already drunk.

They were relaxed too, at ease with each other. The past few days had broken down whatever reservations they may have had about one another. Casually they chatted in short ungrammatical sentences, while unconsciously they waited for Crooke to explain the situation. Finally he wiped his fingers on a clump of grass and said:

'We've made quite a find, you know.'

'How do you mean?'

'Well, in my years in the Middle East, I've heard of two oases which have dried up. A tragedy for the desert Arabs, of course. But to find a new oasis – I've never heard of anyone finding one and never read of such a find in the literature either.'

He dipped his palm in the water can and took a sip.

'You know that the Sahara is constantly developing outwards from the centre. That's the theory at least. This was once the great bread basket of the ancient world, tremendously fertile; that's why the Pharaohs were so tremendously wealthy. Then a combination of changing trade winds and the Romans, who chopped down the cedar forests all along the coast of the Med for their fleets, altered the whole situation. The rains washed away the humus from the fields and left behind the rock and over the centuries the rocks turned into sand.'

'But apart from the water for people like us, how does that make an oasis like this so important?' Stevens asked.

'Because they are so rare out here. There's always talk about them in scientific and business circles. They want to turn them into a base for something else, changing back the whole process, for instance, trying to force the desert back.'

He warmed to his subject. Above them the plateau was silent. Whatever, or whoever was up there, made no noise.

'We know, for example, that there are

great pools of what is called "fossilized water" under the surface of the desert, but pretty deep. Where those pools are and how deep they are have been kept secret by those in the know. The oil companies out prospecting the desert before the war even made their people sign a secrecy clause that they wouldn't reveal what they knew of the "fossilized water" reserves they might have found during their research. The reason was simple. One day the water might prove more valuable than the oil itself.'

He paused and allowed them to absorb the information.

'That perhaps explains what happened out here in '37. It might have run something like this. The three of them – El Nouri, Youngblood and the Count found this place. Plenty of excitement naturally. But if that wasn't enough they climbed up that cliff behind us and possibly found more water. Whatever it was they were all hotfoot to get back to Cairo and tell the authorities there the world-shaking news – at least, world-shaking for the academics and the financial people who might have been prepared to put up money to do something about exploiting the find. There are enough of them still in the capital who think the desert can be transformed into a Garden of Eden again. But they had hardly got started on their way back when they began quarrelling. Perhaps it started about who should have the honour of the discovery. Youngblood might have wanted to claim it for the Empire. It's reasonable in view of his background. Nouri wanted the honour for his own little group of hotheads perhaps – to propagate the idea of a *new Egypt,* and the Count? Who knows? At all events, one word led to another. The result was what you saw out there.'

'But they wouldn't go as far as murder, sir, would they?' Peters asked.

Crooke laughed.

'Wouldn't they! You don't know your explorers and academics, your professors, Peters! Read the history of some of the great discoveries in the Middle East since the time of Schliemann onwards and you'll find that learned men who normally look as if they couldn't say boo to a goose will murder at the drop of a hat if it comes to having to protect their "great discoveries".'

'But what happened to Kraut then? How did he get away?' asked Jones.

'Well, it's obvious he didn't attempt to go back to their starting point. He wasn't spotted in Cairo again until he turned up as a member of the *Brandenburg* group.'

'So?'

Crooke looked at the dark cliff behind them with its silent plateau.

'At dawn we'll start on up there to find out. The answer lies somewhere on that plateau.'

Gippo looked up at the dark threatening flank of the cliff towering above them and gave an audible shudder. The group relaxed into a broody silence, their happy mood gone.

Just before dawn they began their climb. The cliff was easy, but the thick camel scrub which lined its slopes was murderous, tearing and ripping at their bare knees as they stumbled and cursed in the darkness.

'A little less noise,' Crooke ordered, gingerly pulling another long thorn from his leg. 'The Count is no Egyptian. He's probably smart enough to put out sentries, even this far down.'

They found proof that Crooke was right a quarter of an hour later. Armed with the two shovels and the jack they had found in the ancient truck, they were marching in single file down a narrow gully when they almost stumbled into the first sentry asleep in a ring of boulders about three feet above the track.

'There,' Stevens whispered urgently and stopped so abruptly that the guardsman almost bumped into him, 'a Gippo sentry. If we rush him from in front, he'd get one of us before we got him.'

The American looked down in disgust at the shovel he was carrying.

'What the hell can ya do with this piece of crap!'

'Let me have a go, sir.' It was Peters. Ever since they had found the skeleton of Colonel Youngblood there was a new resolution in him, a new iron in his soul, as if he had come to terms with the bloody business of war.

'I'll shin up there.' He pointed to a narrow path running up and above the sentry's position, just vaguely to be seen in the dirty white light of dawn. 'And I'll come down behind him.' He gripped the jack handle he was carrying significantly. Crooke knew they couldn't afford to take any chances now. One warning shot – even a scream from the lone sentry – and they would be exposed on the cliff side, sitting ducks even for the notoriously poor shots of the Egyptian army.

'Are you sure?'

'I'm sure, sir.'

Swiftly he slipped away. Crouched in the path they watched him as he felt his way cautiously along the cliff wall, his back turned towards them, his fingers searching for handholds. Once he slipped and there was a slight fall of rubble. To them, crouched there, holding their breath, it seemed more like a landslide. Anxiously they stared at the spot where the sentry was sleeping behind his wall of boulders, their hearts thumping. But he did not move.

As Crooke breathed out a long sigh of relief, the guardsman pulled himself up again and passed on to vanish from their sight, hidden in a fold in the rock just above the sentry.

In the thin white light, Peters could see every detail of the sleeping man's face. He was a skinny teenager, who had probably joined the army to be struck by the typical, brutal Egyptian NCO and sworn at, and spat at by his middle-class officers in order to escape the grinding poverty of his Cairo slum. Now he was going to die because he had pressed his thumbprint on the entry form to what he thought was going to be the ticket for three square meals for the rest of his mature life.

Slowly and carefully Peters began to climb down the side of the cliff. The Egyptian stirred. Dully and with terrible slowness he started to move his dark greasy head. Obviously he had heard the noise of the guardsman's boots on the rock. Suddenly he opened his eyes and saw Peters poised above him the jack raised in his hand. He opened his mouth to scream. Too late! The guardsman hit him hard with the iron jack. He heard the skull crack. He hit him again. The Egyptian pitched forward without a sound. He was dead.

Minutes later the little group were sharing out the spoils – an old Lee Enfield rifle of Great War vintage and fifty rounds, an overlong bayonet which went with it and to their surprise a gleaming new MG 42, the latest model Spandau, which was perched on the rocks, surrounded by long gleaming belts of cartridge.

The American cradled the heavy weapon in his arms and looked at it almost lovingly as if it were a child and he a proud mother. 'Can I have this, sir?' he asked Crooke.

Crooke grinned. It was the first time Jones had ever called him 'sir'.

'Yes, you can have it.'

'Thank you.' He drew the words out. 'Boy, ain't she a beaut; better than that goddam bren.' He revelled in his strange, almost pathological, attraction to weapons of death and destruction.

'Why the hell don't yer take it to bed, with yer!' Stevens snorted. He had armed himself with the long bayonet while Crooke had taken the rifle, slinging the bandolier over his shoulder.

The American, drooling over the machine gun, ignored him.

Crooke pushed on, his mind full of the gun, too, but for other reasons. How the devil did a brand new MG 42 come to be in the middle of an uncharted region of the Egyptian desert? The moment they solved one mystery others immediately cropped up to take its place.

Half an hour later, with the sun coming up, Crooke halted them and gave them five minutes break. The top of the cliff was only a matter of a hundred yards away and he wanted them to be fresh when they reached it. God alone knew what they would find up there.

Crooke sat down among the boulders, his mind running over the manifold possibilities, but none seemed to make sense. He would wait until they had reached the top. That would solve the whole damned mystery once and for all, he told himself. He put the subject out of his mind and started searching the sky with his one eye. There was no sign of the little spotter plane. If the Fieseler Storch located them now it would be sheer slaughter.

He was just about to order them to move on when his eye fell on the crude frieze cut in the rock opposite him. It depicted tall obviously black warriors – their bodies filled in with black dye – fighting other warriors, similarly armed with spears. The frieze, which ran the whole length of the flat rock face, depicted some ancient battle for a waterhole, for in its middle there was a crude but recognizable depiction of a palm tree. Crooke smiled at it. Eight thousand years old perhaps, when people still inhabited this part of the world and even then man was fighting for the same old things. Nothing seemed to change.

Crooke rose to his feet and picked up the Lee Enfield. He slipped off the safety catch. There was no time now for fancy philosophical thoughts about the futility of human existence. They had to push on.

Twenty minutes later they breasted the top of the cliff and dropped among the boulders scattered on the parched grass and sand, panting with the effort.

Before them stretched a great curved sweep of almost perfectly flat plain, running to the little clumps of palms and bushes which almost hid the tented camp set up among them. But it wasn't the trees nor the red swastika flag which hung limply in their midst that excited their attention. Nor did their wide, round staring eyes linger on the little Fieseler Storch parked behind the camp. It was the great man-made object in the foreground to which they were all drawn as if by a gigantic magnet.

'Christ, will ya just look at that!' the American breathed, awe-stricken.

He pointed to the plane, which was almost assembled, its four engines gleaming in the sun, dwarfing the two sentries wearing the peaked caps of the *Afrika Korps,* who stood guard over it.

'A ruddy Condor,' Stevens said.

'And that, my lad,' said Crooke, 'is the way the Count is going to get the General out – *and more!*'

2

'It all fits together now,' Crooke said as they lay concealed in the rocks at the edge of the plateau and watched two Germans and a dozen or so Egyptian helpers hammer away at the four-engined plane, which was clearly almost ready to fly.

'When they knew they hadn't a chance of getting El Nouri out any other way, they decided to use this way out – a third back door to Libya none of our Intelligence people, even Commander Mallory, ever dreamed of. And why should they? Who would have thought of an airstrip a thousand odd miles south of Cairo, in the middle of the desert?'

'But all this, just for the sake of the Gippo General,' Stevens objected. 'Pull the other leg, sir. It's got bells on it.'

Crooke shook his head. 'Of course not. There's more to it than that. That plane is only the first of them. Look at those parachutes to the rear of the tents next to those two trucks.' They followed the direction of his gaze and stared at the heap of carelessly folded parachutes and beyond them two great trucks, equipped with enormous sand tyres that reached right up to their high cabs.

'That's where the Gippos got their scarves from,' Stevens said.

'Yes, para drops. The Fieseler Storch obviously supplied the Count on the last stage of his escape from Cairo. It could be, too, that the range of the Condor is great enough to enable it to get down as far as this from – say – Derna Airfield. But I doubt it.' He pointed to the two trucks. 'Those Citroens were the ones which brought the parts of the plane they're assembling down here.'

Hastily he explained that the French in Algeria had developed the special desert vehicles after the success of their great Trans-Sahara expedition, during which they used the prototype of the Citroen, in 1928. 'They can each carry a crew and a load of up to ten tons – even across soft sand. Two of them together, supplied by para as they crossed the two thousand kilometres between here and the nearest Italian outpost, could have managed to get the parts here in separate sections.'

The little group of soldiers, lying in the sand, surveying the busy workers around the plane, were impressed. 'I must say something for you Jerries,' Stevens cracked to Thaelmann, 'you certainly know how to get your fingers out when it comes to graft. Them two blond lads are gonna rupture themselves, the way they are going at it.'

Thaelmann grunted a rude answer in his usual morose manner.

'And your mother,' Stevens answered, in no way put out by the drastic and unsanitary suggestion as to what he could do.

Crooke continued, 'What they've done once, they can do again. They've probably got several score of those big Citroens at their disposal, looted from the French in North Africa, each capable of towing the same load.'

'But what for?' Stevens asked.

Crooke did not answer for a moment. A couple of Egyptian soldiers were climbing into a dusty Bedford truck which was parked beyond the camouflaged pup tents of the German *Afrika Korps* men, who numbered about a dozen. Obviously, Crooke thought, there was another way to the high plateau which could be reached by vehicle. Another two Egyptians, rifles slung over their shoulders, were fixing heavy tyres by ropes to the back of the truck. He watched them curiously for a further minute or two. Then he continued.

'Probably when the Count killed the other two in '37 and knew he couldn't go back to Cairo, somehow or other he struggled to the nearest Italian oasis at Kufrah, which they had taken off the Senussi tribe in the early thirties when they started to penetrate deeper into the Libyan desert. From there they might well have shipped him back to Germany.' He licked his lips and watched as the Bedford started to drive through the tented camp. 'But our friend was in a fix. There was no chance of his turning up in Cairo again. He'd burnt his boats there well and truly. But God knows what he did in those pre-war years in Germany. No one would have been even faintly interested in his discoveries out here. But with the advent of war all that changed, even more when the Eyties got themselves involved and the desert war started. Once Rommel got into the act and tried to bail the Italian Army out of the mess it had got itself into, people like Count Kun became highly important.'

'I can see that, Lootenant, but why all this fuss out here? You can't win the war a thousand K's from the front.'

Crooke smiled. 'I wonder. Rommel's a cunning old fox. We've been in Egypt over half a century and think we know all about it, but Rommel learned more in a year than we have in fifty. When we stuck to the old coastal road on offensive actions – I'm not talking of the LRDG now – but major units, brigades, divisions and the like, *he* plunged into the desert, not far, but deep enough to turn our flank. When we caught on, Rommel dreamed up a back door that no one else has ever opened – that our people don't even know is there. What if at the same time that he gets El Nouri to do his bit to bring out the Gippo Army in our rear and on our lines of communication, a battalion – just one highly trained battalion – of the best troops Jerry has out here also came in through the backdoor? *This backdoor!*'

He let the words sink in. By now the Bedford had cleared the camp and was heading slowly in their direction.

'Just eight hundred men, but trained, tough and ruthless. They'd stiffen the Gippos and turn the whole balance – whether the British Empire continues to exist or not.'

Thaelmann looked at him curiously, as if

204

he were seeing the one-eyed officer in his true colours for the very first time. But he said nothing. As usual it was the Cockney Stevens who did the questioning.

'But how would they get in a battalion through the desert, sir? Eight hundred men all that way from Kufrah. It'd take a heck of a long time to get that lot here by truck. And when they had them here, how are they gonna get into the Delta to back up the Gippo Army?'

'Yes, yes, I agree,' Crooke said hastily. He indicated the Bedford. Slowly the Egyptian truck, with two soldiers standing, legs astraddle on the heavy tyres, was advancing on the expanse of plain some five hundred yards away from them. The driver stopped, engaged first gear noisily and then began to drive up and down the area, sending up a great cloud of dust which almost obscured the two soldiers balanced precariously on the tyres.

'There's your answer and the idea our friend the Count must have sold the Germans to get them to send him out here. A runway. The Germans have sailed an aircraft carrier right up to our back door and we don't even know it's there. Now all they're waiting for is for the flightdeck to be cleared so that they can get ready for the big strike.'

But Crooke was fated to be wrong.

'I may not be awful smart, Lootenant,' the American said lazily, as he lay there among the burning rocks, still cradling the MG42 in his arms, 'but I kinda think that those two coons over there on the back of that vehicle have picked themselves a real nice way of getting themselves a snazzy wooden over-coat.'

'Come again, Yank?' the Cockney queried.

'Hell, can't ya speak English?' snarled Jones, 'Getting themselves knocked off – *killed!*'

Crooke eased his position among the rocks and wiped the sweat off his face for the thousandth time.

'Yes, you're right, but perhaps not the way you think.'

'How's that?'

'You'd like to give them one burst of that,' he indicated the long barrel of the Spandau. 'I know you, Jones. But what then?'

'I can tell you, sir,' Thaelmann broke into the conversation. 'We have five hundred metres – er, yards – of open ground to cover. Six of us, armed with a poor collection of weapons. They'd mow us down like that.'

Stevens chimed in. 'The Jerry's right, sir. We're in trouble. Six of us and about six Jerries at least down there and a couple of dozen Gippos.'

Crooke nodded. 'We wouldn't have a chance with the weapons at our disposal. I discount the Egyptians, however. The Germans are our problem, and they'd pick us off before we even got within spitting distance. There's not one bit of cover out there until you reach the palms. There is a way, though.'

'You mean the truck out there?' Stevens asked.

'Yes. You know the Egyptians? As soon as the sun reaches its zenith, they're going to get their heads down for a kip. Now when those fellows out there' – he indicated the truck still making its way back and forth in its cloud of dust – 'pack up, let's hope they do so out here and don't go back to the camp. If they do stay out here,' he paused and struck a clenched fist hard into the palm of the other hand, 'then we've got them by the short and curlies!'

'And then what, when we've got their truck?' the American asked.

'As soon as it starts getting dark and the

men can't work anymore, we head for the camp as if we're finished for the day. We head straight for El Nouri's tent and that of the Count. Once we have them in our hands as hostages, the rest will fold up, believe you me – even the Germans. Without them, the group is helpless. How do they get out of this place otherwise?'

'The plane?' Stevens suggested.

'I doubt it,' Crooke said. 'It doesn't look ready to me yet. No, I reckon that the only way out for them is the trucks and the only person who can guide them is the Count himself. Without him they're dead pigeons.'

That seemed to satisfy the little band and they settled down behind the cover of the boulders, watching the sun climb higher and higher in the sky.

Crooke had just ordered that they break out their water and dates, preparatory to eating their own frugal midday meal, when across at the camp the hammering stopped. He glanced up.

The two Germans had dropped their tools and were walking back to their camouflaged pup tents. The Egyptians in the truck needed no second invitation. It halted almost immediately. Wearily the two men standing on the tyres dropped from their precarious perches, caked in white dust from head to foot, and walked stiffly to the shade of a few stunted palms. The driver put the truck into gear and followed them.

Swiftly Crooke whispered an order. The men took a hasty pull at the luke-warm, brackish water and slung their waterbottles again.

'All right,' he whispered, 'let's go.'

The American grinned cheerfully at the prospect of action again. 'Roger, Loot-enant,' he said, slipping off the safety-catch on the MG 42 and draping two gleaming belts of ammo around his shoulders.

Gippo grabbed his long, old-fashioned bayonet. All morning he had been sharpening it with almost Oriental fatalism, plunging it time and again into the sand. One by one, like hungry wolves, seeking their prey, they slipped out of the boulders and edged their silent way towards the unsuspecting Egyptians, now eating their white beans from British Army mess-tins.

In five minutes it was all over. One Egyptian, his hand still clutching his Army hardtack biscuit, lay sprawled face down in the sand, Gippo's bayonet protruding from his shoulders, a thin trickle of blood coming from the side of his mouth. Another sat groaning and holding his face which was already beginning to swell up at an enormous rate where the American had hit him with the ammo belt as he tried to reach for his rifle. The other two, still covered in dust, sat, backs pressed rigidly against the rocks, their brown faces sickly white, thin hands stuck straight up in the air.

Gippo dug out his bayonet, then pulled the half-eaten biscuit from his victim's lifeless hand and began eating it. Peters shook his head in disbelief at such lack of personal discipline and picked up one of the Egyptian's rifles, dropping his jack.

Crooke and the American examined the back of the truck. Another three rifles, a pistol and an assorted collection of knives came to light. The American opened a metal ammunition box – it looked as if it had once contained 37 mm shells. It was filled to the brim with German stick grenades, heavy, clumsy-looking, but deadly effective bombs, much superior to the British Mills bombs.

'Goddam,' he said, half in disgust, half in admiration. 'Ain't that typical of them crazy coons! Do a job like that with a box of pineapples in the back of the truck! And primed too. Hell, they could have gone up any darn minute.' He shook his head. 'Boy, aren't they something for the book?'

Crooke smiled. 'Thank God the Egyptians are so stupid. Those grenades are just what we wanted. All of us are armed now. This is just the little bit of extra firepower we're going to need today.'

For an hour they watched the tented camp. Once they saw El Nouri Pasha walk out of his tent and urinate among the palms. But for the most part there was little movement. Even the Germans had apparently adopted the Egyptian siesta, driven to their little two-man tents by the intense midday heat.

About three they began emerging into the open, yawning and stretching their arms, as if they had just awakened from a deep sleep. The Germans splashed water in their faces. Crooke licked his dry lips enviously. Then they strolled lazily over to the Condor. A few minutes later the sound of hammering floated across the plateau. Crooke nodded to Gippo.

'All right, Gippo, tell them to get on the tyres again.' He indicated the two sullen, fearful, dust-covered Egyptian soldiers. 'You,' he said in Arabic to the soldier with the wounded face. 'You get behind the wheel.' He turned to Gippo again. 'You get in the cab beside him and keep him covered. The rest of you in the back and keep down. We'll give it a few turns back and forth and then when we're close to the camp, we'll drive slowly towards it. Our objective is the big bell tent. That's El Nouri's.'

In the truck it was burning-hot. The floor was agony to touch, but the men lay there in silence and stared out at the grim frightened faces of the two Egyptians on the tyres, as they became wreathed in thick clouds of dust once more.

'Gawd, what a ruddy caper!' Stevens coughed as the dust flew into his mouth. 'A real Fred Karno's.'

'There are many who do that for a living a life-time long,' Thaelmann said solemnly, misunderstanding Stevens and indicating the two Egyptians bouncing up and down three or four feet away from them. 'Exploitation. It is the nature of capitalist society.'

'Aw hell, Kraut, you're a real ray of sunshine,' Jones said good-humouredly, happy at the prospect of action. 'Knock it off.'

'Save your breath,' Crooke snapped, lying on the floor, his head a foot away from the American's boots. 'You'll be needing it soon.' He raised his voice above the roar of the motor.

'Gippo! Let's make our way to the camp now.'

'Righty ho, sir,' Gippo said cheerfully and finished the rest of his beans unhurriedly. Gippo had the eating habits of a camel: he ate his fill – and more – whenever he had the opportunity, preparing for the day when there was nothing to eat.

He jabbed the bayonet in the driver's side.

'Nice and slow,' he ordered in Arabic. The man lifted his foot slightly from the accelerator. Slowly they started to approach the unsuspecting camp and its busy occupants.

Peeping out of the back, Crooke could see the great sand-camouflaged shape of the four-engined reconnaissance plane loom up ahead. The two mechanics were obviously about finished. A man, naked to the waist – perhaps an NCO – was giving orders to one of the Germans poised at the propeller of one of the port engines. It looked as if they were going to try the engines; an auxiliary starting motor was already in position under the nose.

His one eye fixed on the activities of the mechanics, Crooke did not hear the soft airborne swish of the newcomers until it was too late. Abruptly a great green shape blocked out the view in front of the truck's windscreen. It hushed into land with a grinding scream of air brakes and protesting wooden fuselage. The driver, shocked by the sudden apparition, hit the brakes. Gippo grabbed the wheel.

'*What the hell!*' somebody shouted.

Behind them the two prisoners dropped off the wheels, and started to run for the palms. There was a short burst of machine-gun fire and they flung up their skinny arms and flopped down in the sand, their bodies sawn almost in half.

'GLIDERS!' Crooke yelled hysterically. Above him, at not more than fifty feet, another gigantic plane was coming in to land. Way above, a dark dot against the blinding blue sky droned on. The tug was another Condor. In a flash everything was confusion and chaos. The first glider – a DFS 230, as he identified it later – touched down. It slewed to the right. The pilot caught it in time. It straightened up, and bounced twenty feet into the air again. A second later it made a grinding, rending landfall. Two thousand pounds of men and glider hit the plateau twenty yards in front of them. The barbed wire wrapped around its skids to cut the landing distance snapped like twine. Swaying and shuddering, one wing splintered like matchwood as it struck a palm, it staggered to a standstill in a thick cloud of dust.

For a moment no one moved, either in the truck or the plane. Then the door of the glider flew off. Crooke snapped himself out of his trance. Now they'd have to fight for their lives.

'Let the bastards have it!' he roared, as the men started to tumble out.

What happened next was not war, but murder – the sheer pitiless massacre of the defenceless figures in the faded khaki of the *Afrika Korps*. Instead of being greeted by shouts of welcome and the handshakes of their comrades on the ground, they were met by a wall of fire. Uncomprehending, stunned and confused by this terrible thing happening to them, they spun and collapsed like marionettes in the hands of a puppet-master, suddenly gone crazy.

Most of them lay where they fell. Others tried frantically to fight their way out of the bloody mess of dead and dying men jammed in the door. The American crouched over his Spandau did not give them a chance. He poured a whole belt into them. Screaming and yelling at the tops of their voices, legs and arms flailing as they were hit over and over again at such a short range, they dropped on the grotesquely stacked bodies of their comrades.

A few fled back into the plane, but they were not to live for long.

'*Jones,*' Crooke cried above the screams and futile cries of *Sanitäter* by the dying Germans. No medics would ever come to their aid.

'*Lootenant!*'

Crooke caught a glimpse of the American's happy face. The man was born a killer. He brought up his Spandau again. 'The back of the plane!' he ordered.

'*Wilco!*' the American pressed the trigger. The gun burst into its high-pitched song of death once more. The bullets stitched a long line along the fuselage to the tail and back again. Screams rose from within.

Stevens grabbed one of the long-handled 'potato-mashers' from the ammo box. Hastily he pulled the string at the base. The pin came out easily. He drew a deep breath and flung it. It somersaulted through the air and sailed in through the door packed at floor-level with the dead and dying, and exploded with a muffled crump. The canvas fuselage flew apart and began to burn.

The American took his finger off the

216

trigger. 'We got the buggers!' he cried almost joyously. 'We got the buggers!' But Crooke knew no triumph, no pleasure. From the camp came the shrill whistles of the NCOs and the angry shouts of the Egyptians. The German technicians had dropped behind the big plane and opened fire. Bullets started to whistle their way. That wasn't all. The second glider had somersaulted to a stop among the palms, its wings snapped off and its broken tail high in the air. Men were pouring out of it unimpeded and were racing for cover – perhaps fifty of them – and all armed! With a sinking feeling he shouted, 'All right, out of the truck... At the double!'

There was a rush to get out. In front of them the glider was burning furiously and its black smoke offered them temporary cover.

'Back to the boulders,' Crooke yelled. 'And make it fast. We're in real trouble now.'

3

The single light German mortar hidden behind the palms to their right gave one last obscene belch. There was a frightening whistle. A moment later a huge hole appeared to their front. They cowered among the boulders as sand and stones showered down upon them. Then there was silence. Stevens raised his head and peered out. The ground in front of them was pockmarked with great holes made by the mortar bombs. The glider, completely burnt out now, lay filled with charred bodies, as if some monster had set a gigantic birdcage on fire.

A minute passed and another and another. They watched their front intently. Even the American was silent as he crouched over his machine-gun, half-a-dozen stick grenades wedged securely on the rock in front of him.

Then they came. In little bunches, running awkwardly through the palms, their bayonets at their hips. They were not more than fifty yards away now, at least fifty of them. They came out on to the naked plateau, bare of cover. *Why didn't Crooke give the order to fire?* They threw a glance at their commander, captured pistol in his hand, standing upright in spite of the obvious danger. He was motionless.

The enemy was almost on them. They could see every detail of the German officer's face quite clearly now, as he hurried on at the head of his men, his pistol clasped tightly to his hip. They could make out the silver stars on his shoulders and the untidy lock of white blond hair escaping from under the side of his peaked cap.

'*NOW!*' Crooke shouted at the top of his voice.

Their first volley crashed into the advancing Brandenburgers tearing murderous holes in their ranks. And another. The German commander was hit. He clutched frantically at his chest. Slowly, his legs buckling under him like those of a newborn calf, he began to fall, his hair hanging lankly down from his capless head like that of a schoolboy. All along the ragged lines his comrades were falling too, crying out in agony, cursing with rage as they were flung off their feet by the terrible fire.

When they were only ten yards away the

Germans broke. Suddenly, without a word, they stopped, hesitated, then turned and began running back, dropping their weapons, running with hysterical sobs to the cover of the palms, tramping mercilessly over the dead and dying bodies of their comrades, intent solely on getting away from that murderous hail of lead.

Half-an-hour later they came again, this time running straight at Crooke's position, screaming at the tops of their voices and waving their weapons with hysterical abandon, as if they were drunk or drugged.

'Alles für Deutschland ... alles für den Führer!' they cried over and over again.

In front ran their officers, firing their machine pistols wildly from the hip. Behind them lumbered the rest, slowed down now by the scuffed, bloodied sand and the bodies of the dead from the first charge.

The defenders stopped them at fifty yards. This time Crooke was taking no chances. They broke again and streamed back, racing for the trees, leaving four young officers dead or wounded among the others who littered the plateau.

And yet again they came, this time cautiously, drifting slyly from the cover of

220

the palms in little groups of three or four, directed by an older officer who wore a helmet. They did not seem to be heading straight for the British positions. They were extending more to left and right flanks.

Crooke tumbled to their game in sudden alarm. They were outflanking him!

'Jones,' he yelled. 'Out to the left with your gun! You cover him, Gippo! Stevens, grab a bag of grenades and get out to the right. Stop the bastards *quick*.'

Stevens stuck half-a-dozen grenades in his shirt and doubled, crouched well down, to the threatened flank. He did not arrive a moment too soon. Heavy firing broke out almost at once, followed by the soft muffled crump of the grenades as they exploded in the sand.

It was dangerous now to remain behind the rock wall. The Germans were every-where – to the front, right and left of them. They sprang to their feet and poured fire into the enemy, swinging their weapons to left and right, as they met the full shock of the new attack. Thaelmann standing next to Crooke grunted and sat down abruptly. Blood started to flow from a wounded shoulder. But he was up again the next instant. To their front the Brandenburgers were taking casualties too. But the older officer to their rear was everywhere, springing nimbly from group to group urging them on with waves of his machine pistol. And then the Germans were among them. The air was filled with curses and cries in German as the fire slackened in the centre and a bitter man-to-man struggle began.

The guardsman struggled with a young thickset German, the two of them swaying back and forth in a macabre parody of the dance, until with a grunt the guardsman let go of the rifle he was trying to wrench from the German's hands. Next instant Peters kicked him between the legs, sending him screaming and vomiting backwards into the nearest mortarbomb hole.

A Brandenburger loomed up in front of Crooke. He pressed his trigger. The pistol clicked. Desperately he swung it back and just as the German was about to drive home his bayonet, thrashed it across the man's face. The blow smashed the German's nose, the bone snapping like a twig. Great gobs of blood flew everywhere, staining Crooke's torn shirt. The soldier dropped instantly, screaming with pain.

Peters dropped suddenly, blood pouring from a shattered kneecap. Two Germans rushed at him as Crooke screamed a warning. But he wasn't finished yet. He grabbed a machine pistol dropped by one of the dead. In a single motion he pressed the trigger and swung the Schmeisser from left to right. The two Germans came to an abrupt halt, blood spurting from the line of holes across their chests.

'Look out!' Thaelmann screamed at Crooke's side.

He spun round to see a gigantic German *Feldwebel* coming at him! He had approached them from the rear, unseen, and in his big hands he held a bayonet. Crooke raised his hands to protect his naked chest against the steel that must now penetrate it. Then Thaelmann was between him and the NCO, shovel raised high, bringing down its sharp blade on the German's skull. He continued to beat the German's face as he slipped to his knees, the bayonet dropping from his fingers. Thaelmann stood swaying over the mutilated body of his fellow countryman, shoulders drooping like those of an old ape, spade covered in red gore, dangling from his hand, bloodied to the wrist. Peters was crawling painfully back to their position, while Jones and Stevens were still firing at the retreating enemy.

During the night the surviving Brandenburgers infiltrated close to their position
and began sniping. A bullet striking the rock
just above Crooke's head and showering
him with splinters was the first indication
that they had managed to get so close
without being spotted.

'Heads down,' he snapped, 'they're sniping
us from the trees.'

The ones still capable of standing needed
no urging. They dropped to the ground next
to Peters whose leg had stiffened painfully
and Thaelmann who was nursing his roughly
bandaged shoulder in numb, morose gloom.

The whine and howl of the ricochets off
the boulders grew more frequent as the
Brandenburgers stepped up the pace,
knowing that at dawn they would have to
retreat from their exposed positions in the
palms. Jones reached for his beloved MG 42
and snorted, 'I'll fix them bastards.'

Crooke grabbed him by the arm in time.

'Save your ammunition,' he ordered.
'You'll need every round tomorrow morning once it's light, believe you me.'

Grumpily the American settled down on
his haunches again.

The minutes ticked by, punctuated by the

steady crack and ping of bullets, which never seemed to let up. As the night sky began to break, revealing the first ugly whitewash of the false dawn, the defenders grew uneasy.

'What the heck are they up to?' Stevens asked.

Peters shrugged and his pale face winced with pain.

'Search me, Y-track. Perhaps they want us to keep our loaves o'bread down.'

Whack! Another slug hit the rock a few inches above their heads, as if to emphasize his point. Instinctively they both ducked a little lower.

'See what I mean?'

'Well, why don't they use the mortar again?'

Again Peters shrugged.

'Don't ask me, I'm not Field Marshal Wavell.'

They lapsed into silence.

But they had not long to wait for the answer to Stevens's question. About an hour after the sniping had started in earnest, Gippo, who had stationed himself on the left extremity of their little defensive line, cried out in hurried alarm. 'Look to your front, sir... *To the front!*' His voice rose hysterically.

Forgetting the snipers' bullets completely,

Crooke poked his head over the top of the boulders. A handful of Germans were advancing cautiously from the palms, black outlines against the white of the dawn. Two of them were armed with rifles; behind them came the old officer with the machine pistol. But it wasn't those three who caught Crooke's attention. His eye was fixed on the last man, who moved forward under the cover of the others, weighed down with something that looked like a cumbersome old-fashioned rolled pack.

'Oh, my bloody Christ!' Stevens groaned at his side.

Crooke felt fear well up within him, as he recognized it too.

Abruptly that terrible vision of Mr Brady which had haunted him as a child flashed through his mind with frightening clarity. Ever since he had been able to remember, Mr Brady, a friend of his father's, had worn a thick black bandage over his head which extended low and covered both his ears. As a five-year-old, he had asked his father about it but the latter had dismissed his query with a laconic, 'He got hurt in the big war.' And that had been that. Once he had run into the house unexpectedly and had burst in to find Mr Brady without the black bandage. The man's completely bald head had been a frighteningly bright pink, flecked with small patches of dark brown, horribly wrinkled and puckered like the head of some ancient Egyptian mummy, unwrapped from its bandages after three thousand years under the earth. But worst of all, where the ears should have been, there had been nothing but two dark holes from which the brown wax had escaped unchecked. His father seeing his shocked face had whispered an urgent 'bandage' to Mr Brady and had said 'It's nothing, nothing.'

Hastily the mutilated man had bound up his head once more, but he had not forgotten that terrible sight and for months afterwards it had haunted his dreams. Now he was facing up to the horror of his childhood in reality. Mr Brady's ears had been burned off by a flame-thrower on the Somme in '16. The man with the strange-looking pack was equipped with that most terrible of modern weapons!

He pulled himself together by an effort of will. Banishing the horror from his mind, he shouted:

'They've got a flame-thrower!'

Forgetting the snipers, they raised them-selves and started firing furiously at the little group. But their aim was too hasty. The word 'flame-thrower' had had its effect.

The Germans redoubled their efforts. The volume of their fire increased. The little group began to run, with the flame-thrower hidden in their centre, his pack bouncing up and down clumsily as he ran with them. They pumped shot after shot at them. One of the guards threw up his arms, dropped his rifle and fell to the ground. The rest stopped. The officer shouted something. The flame-thrower moved from behind him, nozzle held in his two hands. He pressed the trigger.

For a moment nothing happened. Suddenly there was a great hushed intake of air. A tongue of purple, oil-tinged flame shot out seventy-five feet. The sand shrank in its path, turning black. The tip of its tongue licked the rocks. They dropped hurriedly. Before their terrified faces the boulders turned a glowing red. The heat was tremendous. It dragged the very breath from their lungs.

Crooke felt the bile rise in his throat. He knew with terrible finality that it was up to him to do something.

Again the long tongue of flame licked out at them greedily like some predatory monster, searching blindly for its petrified prey. The heat engulfed them again. Crooke felt the hair on his head singe. There was the stink of burning hair.

'Bugger this for a tale,' Stevens screamed, *'I'm off.'* He attempted to rise and run.

The American kicked him in the shin.

He dropped heavily, yelping with pain.

Thaelmann grabbed a grenade. In one and the same motion he pulled the pin and lobbed it over the boulders. It exploded harmlessly, twenty feet away from the little group around the flame-thrower.

The man pulled the trigger again. Flame seared the sand and engulfed them. Crooke's mouth opened like a fish on land gasping in its death throes. The heat wrapped itself around them. Again there was the stink of burning hair. Crooke screamed with fear and rage.

'NOW!' he roared. *'NOW, YOU BAS-TARDS!'*

Before anyone could stop him, he sprang on the still glowing rock in front of him, pistol in his hand. Bullets hit the sand and rock all around him. Every remaining German sniper among the palms directed his fire on the lone British officer in the bloodied, torn shirt.

Under the cover of the flame the little

group had advanced to within twenty yards of their positions. This time when the Brandenburger pulled the trigger of his terrible weapon, they would be burned to death.

Suddenly Crooke was terribly calm. An icy wave of absolute certainty swept over him. He raised his captured Walther. The Germans stared at him without movement. Then they realized the danger. The older officer in the helmet screamed something, raising his machine pistol to indicate the British officer standing on the top of the rock.

The flame-thrower raised his nozzle. He looked supremely confident. Nothing could stop him 'flaming' the Englishman now. Slowly, almost pleasurably, his forefinger curled around the big trigger behind its square metallic guard.

Crooke raised his pistol. He stood there against the blood-red light of the sun which had appeared like a ball on the horizon as if he were on some pre-war pistol range. He took careful aim, his one blue eye staring along the barrel.

The German started to squeeze the trigger. In a moment the foolish *Engländer* would be gone, a shrunken charred mass reduced to the size of a child by the killing heat.

Crooke fired first. He hit the flame-thrower first time. In the instant of the impact the German swung round, his finger tightening on the trigger at the same moment. A thick oily stream of flame hit the older officer. He screamed hideously. As the flame-thrower sank into the sand, the officer disappeared too, his helmet glowing dully.

For a few moments the flame-thrower gasped on the sand like some mortally wounded animal next to its dead owner, shrivelling up the ground around it. Then it died.

This marked the end to the Branden-burgers' final attack. The handful of survivors fled back to the tented camp. The sniping stopped. A sudden silence descended upon the battlefield. Stevens licked his dry cracked lips and croaked in hoarse admiration at the officer who was clambering stiffly down from the rock, his one eye fixed on the suddenly still scene of death.

'A bloody good officer, eh, Yank?'

Jones looked at Crooke with almost animal devotion and whispered in awe, 'They ... they don't make 'em like that anymore, Y-track. He's a great guy.'

4

One hour after the failure of the final attack of the Brandenburgers, Stevens, who was standing guard behind the rocks, turned and said urgently to Crooke.

'Sir, there's somebody waving a white flag among the trees.'

Wearily, Crooke opened his eyes and rose slowly to his feet.

'Where?'

'Over there.' Stevens pointed to where one of the palms lay snapped off by the mortar barrage.

Crooke shaded his eyes. 'It's the Count!'

'I wonder what the hell he wants,' Stevens asked.

'Let's find out,' Crooke replied.

Slowly, a dirty piece of white cloth attached to a pick-handle, the Count advanced upon them, limping painfully around the holes of the mortar shells and picking his way gingerly over the dead Brandenburgers already beginning to swell and stink in the heat.

Crooke let him get within twenty yards of

their position before he cried, 'That's far enough! Another step and we'll drop you!'

The Count's face twitched as if he had been struck and he stopped.

'I'd like to speak with you, Mister Crooke.'

'All right, get on with it.'

'You know your position here is hopeless. You are greatly outnumbered still. And even if you did break out tonight when the sun goes down, what would you do – where would you go? You have no water, no food, no vehicle. You haven't a chance.'

'So *you* say,' Crooke answered non-committally. 'But you didn't come out here to tell me that, did you?'

The Count wrinkled his long nose with distaste at the overpowering odour of flesh beginning to decay.

'I must admit that you have one advantage,' he declared. 'You cover the runway.' He gestured to the Condor. 'Quite probably we should not be able to take off while you cover the strip.'

Suddenly the Count shivered violently and could not go on for a minute. The defenders watched him curiously.

'What's up with him?' Peters asked. 'Has he got malaria?'

But the answer was known only to the

Count, who knew he must have the needle again soon, that terrible needle which had dominated his life these past twenty years. Admiral Canaris had gone so far as to consult the Fuehrer's own doctor, the gross Doctor Morell, before they had let him go on the mission. He had discussed the matter with Hitler and the latter had decreed he should have the drug till his task was completed. Then it would be the *'Kur'* for him.

Abruptly he pulled himself together and continued, 'We could wait another day until you decided to give up, which you would. No one could stand his heat another twenty-four hours without water. Not even you, Mister Crooke.'

Crooke said nothing, but he knew the Count was right. Once their water ran out – which would be soon – the resolution would ebb from them. Then they would be pleading to be allowed to surrender.

'I'll make you an offer, however, Mister Crooke. Time is running out. General Field Marshal Rommel radioed us an hour ago that he wants El Nouri Pasha at his headquarters within the next twenty-four hours. I'm telling you this so you will understand the reason for my offer. It is very simple.

Surrender to me and you'll fly with us – all of us. The Condor is big enough. We shall land you at the Senussi oasis – some five hundred miles away – to refuel.'

Crooke's mind registered the incidental information. So that was how they had done it? The Condor towing the two gliders had obviously brought them from the coast. It had landed for refuelling at the Senussi oasis and thus extended its range another thousand miles. The Germans wouldn't use trucks to bring in their Brandenburgers. The key to this back-door into Egypt was the Condor glider-tows. How simple. It would cut the time needed to bring in a battalion to a day at the most, even with a stop for refuelling. This was a tremendous piece of information the Count had revealed to them. They would need it at GHQ, Cairo immediately. There was only one small problem – how to get it to them.

'There I shall leave you with our authorities,' the Count was saying slowly and precisely. 'In due course they will ensure that you are taken to a prisoner-of-war camp – a German one, not an Italian,' he added hastily. 'I know how you British feel about the cages of our noble Roman allies.' He shrugged. 'It is better than death out

235

here, isn't it?'

'Ay, that's what you say now. More than likely we'll end up with a hole in the back of our heads,' Peters shouted. 'Like yer did to Colonel Youngblood!'

Crooke intervened hastily.

'How do we know that we can trust you?'

But the Count ignored him. The guardsman's accusation seemed to have tripped a lever in his brain and he no longer remembered why he had come to speak to Crooke.

'That was quite different,' he stammered, suddenly coming forward to five yards of their position. 'Youngblood was a fool and young El Nouri a fanatic. Once we had discovered the oasis they had no further time. They had to get back to Cairo and tell the world, spread the great news.' His thin face contorted contemptuously. 'Fame – national pride – public honours – that was all they had in their little minds. But what else was to be found here – for that they had no interest, not the littlest interest.' In his excitement, the words pouring from his thin lips, he was beginning to lose his excellent English. 'I explained to them a dozen times. I pleaded with them – just a little more time, a week, a couple of days, one sole single day.' He waved a needle-scarred arm desperately at them. 'But they wouldn't listen. They had no time – no time for the great glories of the past, the find of the century, indescribably more important than that foolish piece of water they thought so valuable, so absurdly valuable.' He paused for air, wiping away the sweat which was pouring down his forehead.

Crooke, remembering the frieze on the rock, asked slowly, 'What was the other find?'

'Why, the greatest archaeological discovery of this century! More than Tutankhamen, as great as Schliemann's discovery of Troy! The site of Cambyses' last battle. *Here!*'

'And for that you killed them?' Peters said incredulously. 'For that bit o' history!'

'What else was there left for me?' Kun asked simply, as if his action had been the most obvious in the world. 'If they had got back to Cairo, the place would have been filled with fools. They would have come poking and searching around until one of them found it. Someone else would have gained the honour.' His eyes narrowed cunningly. 'You little know just how criminal some of those professors in Cairo are in their search for honour and credit! Believe me, I know!'

'The credit!' Crooke sneered. 'Why, you

are as bad as they are!'

'But I deserved it,' the Count protested. 'After they – er, died – I couldn't go back that way. I crossed five hundred miles of uncharted desert out there.' He pointed to the west. *'Five hundred miles!* Can you imagine what that hell was like on foot in these temperatures, till in the end the Senussi found me and took me to their oasis. Didn't I deserve the credit after that?' He stared at their blank uncomprehending faces. 'My God,' he shrieked, 'will nothing move you!' Frantically he reached into his shirt pocket and pulled something out which glinted brightly in the sun. 'Look at this,' he cried, holding it high above his head like a priest raising the chalice at Mass. *'Gold!* Solid gold – a section from a piece of their armour which I dug up not more than a hundred yards from where I am now standing.'

He tossed it over the barricade of rocks. It landed at Gippo's feet. His eyes sparkled greedily and he bent to pick it up. 'Don't touch it, Gippo,' the guardsman growled. 'It's got the blood of many good men on it.'

And something in Peters's voice made Gippo obey.

'But there's more – much more! Enough gold for all of you, if that is what you wish.

Enough to make you rich, tremendously rich. After the war, I promise you, you will be able to come–'

He never finished his sentence.

'Bugger off, you murderous old sod,' Peters snarled and pressed the trigger of his rifle. A round struck the rock a few feet in front of Kun. Rock splinters showered upwards. The Count fell back, his face a mask of incomprehension; he turned and began walking back the way he had come, blundering blindly over the bodies, muttering to himself all the time.

'Christ,' Stevens breathed in awe, 'he's bonkers. The old boy's gone completely off his nut.'

With a long, tobacco-stained finger, the Count found the vein. His whole body was trembling violently. Every millimetre of his skin seemed to be on fire. He controlled the overwhelming desire to begin scratching – if it didn't stop soon, he would rip the flesh off his body with his bare hands!

Mumbling crazily to himself, flecks of foam at his lips, he readied the needle: that beloved-hated needle. A slight prick of pain. Slowly, luxuriously it sank deep into the vein. He pressed the plunger with his thumb. The liquid began spurting into the vein to start its long journey around his pain-racked body. Although he knew from his doctors that the morphia would take at least five minutes to work, the pain which seared his leg from hip to toe seemed already to be vanishing. He wriggled his toe. There was no spurt of pain which would have been the result only a moment before.

He withdrew the needle and dipped its point in the little bottle of alcohol. Carefully he replaced it in the same worn black case he had bought so long ago in Vienna after they had released him from the *Kriegslazarett*, and he had known then that he would never again be able to live without the needle. He glanced at his ravaged face in the little steel shaving mirror hanging from the tent's centre pole. The red glare had almost gone from his eyes.

Outside the crackle of the snipers in the trees continued. The Egyptians, under El Nouri's personal command, were keeping up the pressure. But the Britishers did not even bother to reply. The Egyptians were notoriously bad shots and Crooke was obviously saving his ammunition.

'Heaven, arse and twine,' Kun cursed to himself in German. 'Why did I let that Englishman get away the first time?' Like

most lonely men, the Count had talked to himself for many years. 'Then I would not be sitting in this damned shit now.'

But his anger was tinged with admiration. The one-eyed lieutenant was typical of the best British colonial officers he had met during his years in Africa: hard, bold men who went their own way, disdaining the common herd.

'Men who are prepared to walk over bodies,' he said aloud using the German expression. 'Jesus Christ, Mary, that one should have to fight against such men!'

He dismissed the thought. There was no time for philosophising about the futility of war now. He must concentrate on the task in hand. His crazy eyes stared back at him from the mirror. He knew his boss, the old fox Admiral Canaris would accept no excuses. He *must* get El Nouri Pasha out!

'When the British are driven out of Egypt,' he told himself, still speaking aloud, 'perhaps they will allow me to devote myself to the plateau. How many years have I got left? Not many. Five at the most. Surely the Old Fox will let me go from the Brandenburgers then!'

He remembered how Canaris had said to him in his bare office in the *Tirpitzufer*, with

241

his two pet poodles sleeping at his feet, on the day he had left for Africa: 'After all my dear Count, we are both getting too old for this business. It is no longer one for gentlemen. Perhaps we should let you go when this mission is completed?'

He sat looking at himself in the mirror while he deliberated on the real meaning of 'perhaps we should let you go'.

By now the drug was taking full effect. The pain had vanished. In addition, in spite of what the doctors said to the contrary, morphia seemed to have a stimulating as well as a pain-killing influence on him. His mind raced. Desperately he sought to find a way out of the impasse. The Brandenburgers were finished. There were only a few of them left after the disastrous attacks on Crooke's position. The Egyptians were little better than useless. They would never break through. Then he had it! It came suddenly, completely, with every last detail worked out, as if somewhere in his sub-conscious, it had been long in the process of planning. He took one last glance at those shining crazy eyes in the little steel mirror and ran out of the tent, as if he could not wait to put the plan into operation.

The Fieseler Storch pilot and crew of the Condor were playing *skat* under the shelter of a canvas awning stretched between the plane and a nearby palm, stripped to the waist and calm, as if they were on some peace-time field and not a hundred yards away from where other men were getting killed. But the four aircrew were typical of the *Luftwaffe,* with their fliers' contempt of the common 'stubble-hoppers', as they called the infantry.

'*Oberleutnant* Duddeck,' Kun snapped.

Duddeck, a sleek-haired plump Berliner rose to report in the German fashion, *skat* card still held in his hand. The Count waved for him to forget the military ritual.

'Duddeck, is your plane ready to take off?'

'*Jawohl, Herr Major.*' He indicated the two crew members. 'I checked everything with Klimek and Huhn here during the night.'

'Could you take off?' he looked anxiously at the distance between the Condor and the landing strip. 'You seem a bit of a way off?'

'No problem whatsoever, *Herr Graf.*' Duddeck shrugged. 'Save one little detail. The Tommies out there behind those rocks could cut us to ribbons before we could get airborne.'

'Thank you, Duddeck.'

There was a moment's silence while the volume of small arms fire from the direction of the palms grew steadily. That would be El Nouri trying to put some steel into the hearts of his waverers.

Kun turned to Eberl, a tough little bow-legged Bavarian, whom General Student, the head of the German paratroops had recommended specially for this mission. Before the war he had been Germany's number one glider pilot. After landing one of the nine gliders which had borne the paras to the astoundingly successful attack on Fort Eben-Emael in Belgium in 1940, he had transferred to the spotter planes. Now two years later he was acknowledged to be Germany's finest Fieseler Storch pilot and the man who was always given the honour of flying Reich Marshal Hermann Goering himself on his inspection of Army troops.

'Eberl, how about you?' he asked. 'Could you take off from this?' He indicated the scuffed, boulder-littered sand behind the palms.

'Sure,' he said confidently. 'This son-of-a-bitch could take off anywhere.' He slapped the Storch's fuselage lovingly. Kun put his hand paternally on the young man's shoulder.

'Will you come with me for a moment. I have something which I'd like to show you.'

The pilot grabbed his forage cap and followed him. In silence they walked to the edge of the palms. The firing had died away again now. In front of them stretched the grass-tufted plateau to where the cliff began.

'What do you estimate is the distance to the edge?' the Count asked.

The pilot screwed up his eyes and made his estimate. In two years of flying Storchs he had got used to this question. All his passengers seemed concerned with distances. Then later when he had put them down safely in some unlikely spot or other, they would boast to their fellow generals over the welcoming *Kognak* in the mess. 'But of course, the man is reputed to be able to put down a Storch on a postage stamp.'

'I'd say about two hundred metres.'

'Do you think you could take off in that distance with a passenger and other extra weight on board?'

'Not impossible, but dicey.' He walked towards the edge of the cliff and the Count followed. Now it was his turn to be mystified. What was the man looking for out there? They came to the deeply fissured edge and the pilot stared down at the brown burning expanse of the desert far below.

'I'd say that's about a thousand feet – to down there, eh?'

'Eleven hundred and fifty to be exact,' the Count answered. 'I measured the height in thirty-seven.'

'I see.' The bow-legged Bavarian absorbed the information, then turned to face the taller man. 'Well under normal circumstances I couldn't get off with a passenger and perhaps other extra weight within two hundred metres. However, if you think it is important, *Herr Graf*, I could try like this.'

Hastily he bent down and drew a rough line in the sand with his fore-finger.

'That's the edge of the date trees, yes? If I could set off from there at full throttle – someone would have to hold the wings till I got power – I might reach sufficient speed to be airborne just as I reached the edge of the cliff.' He drew another line in the sand and looked at it thoughtfully. 'It would be touch and go. But,' he straightened up again and pointed over the edge of the cliff, 'once I was airborne and started losing height – which I would with that weight aboard – I'd drop a couple of hundred feet at least – God willing. I might just catch the bitch again and force her up.' He tapped his temple in the German gesture and said *'unberufen toi, toi'* – touch wood!' He stared down at the rocks far below.

'If I didn't, you could gather my pieces up for *goulasch.*'

The Count seized the pilot's arm.

'Come on, let's get back to Duddeck. I need him too.'

5

'Bloody hell,' Stevens swore, 'I'm parched.' He spat out the pebble in disgust. 'These bloody rocks don't help one sodding bit!' He looked over at the guardsman, his hand clenched around his wounded leg, his face pinched with pain. 'Remember that Charing Cross★ water – that was bloody good, wasn't it?'

The guardsman nodded, but he could not trust himself to speak.

Another bullet whacked against the rock

★Charing Cross Track – highly regarded as a source of good water among the Eighth Army.

above Stevens's head and put an end to that particular attempt at conversation. Crooke rubbed the sweat off his face, the blood from where the rocks splinters had wounded his forehead mixing with it. He looked around the little group of exhausted men sprawled behind the boulders over which the heat haze shimmered. Even Thaelmann, whose wound was beginning to suppurate badly now, grinned at him bravely every time he looked in the German's direction. Yet in spite of the men's toughness and their high morale, he knew they couldn't hold out much longer. The Brandenburgers were no longer a danger. But there were at least a score of Egyptians sniping at them from the trees; they would keep them down till their supplies of ammo and water ran out.

He leaned over to where Peters lay nursing his leg.

'How's the water?' He had given him the job of looking after the water ration.

'One and a half bottles left, sir... Enough for another twelve hours.'

Crooke looked glum. 'How's the ammo?'

'Fair, we've still got half a box of grenades left. But the Yank's nearly out of ammo.'

'There's a bit of a movement at the camp,

Lootenant.' It was Jones who was on look-out.

Crooke rose and crawled cautiously over to where he lay, the blood seeping through the rough bandage, stolen from one of the German dead, which was bound around his head.

'Jones, you look like the fellow in the "Spirit of Seventy-Six",' he said.

'Huh,' the American grunted, 'come again.' He looked at Crooke as if the sun were turning him crazy.

'Forget it,' Crooke said. 'What's going on?'

'Over there,' the American pointed to the tented camp. 'They're getting the Condor pointed towards the runway. Ya think they're gonna try to get the bastard in the air?'

An Egyptian sniper spotted them and a slug smacked into the rock a foot away from them. They ducked. Crooke shook his head.

'Whatever they're up to, they'll never get by us as long as we've got enough ammo to stop them.'

The American's suspicious look disappeared. 'Yeah, I guess ya right. We'd cut the bastards to ribbons before they'd be able to get that bomb into the air.'

Crooke squatted down again and relaxed. Abruptly there was a thick throaty mechanical grunt which died a second later. They stirred vaguely. Then the sound came again, longer this time. A pause, then again – an aero engine bursting into ear-splitting life, shattering the heavy stillness of the desert afternoon. A second later another followed it.

All of them scrambled to the rocks. The Condor was rolling slowly towards the air strip, but still it was not close enough for them to open fire. It would only be a waste of ammunition.

'What the hell are they doing?' Stevens cried.

Seconds later he found out.

The Storch came in low to their rear. The pilot had cut the engine and came gliding in silently. They heard him only when it was too late. Suddenly the little spotting plane was directly overhead. A swish, a roar as Eberl snapped on the engine, and the little black objects came tumbling out of the open cockpit like metal eggs.

'Get down!' Crooke yelled at the top of his voice.

Flinging themselves into the dirt, they buried their faces in their crossed arms.

The first grenade struck the rock a few

feet away and sent red-hot shards of metal winging viciously through the air. It was followed by more. The splinters flew everywhere. Crooke felt a sharp pain in his back. He looked up, just in time to catch a glimpse of the dark figure poised next to the pilot pouring something from a jerry can.

A moment later the light plane had zoomed away and the air was full of the sharp stink of petrol. A hundred yards away the empty jerry can came tumbling down.

'What the hell are those bastards up to—' someone began, but his words were drowned by the noise of the motor. Eberl came roaring in at 150 mph from the opposite direction. Just before he reached them, he pulled up the nose and dropped his flaps. The plane seemed to stop and hover momentarily in mid-air. Eberl was a fine pilot, but Crooke had no time to admire his flying ability.

The grenades came sailing down again. The American swore fluently as a chunk of metal struck him on the naked arm. Stevens was hit too. He pressed himself tightly to the base of a huge boulder, blood pouring from a great gash in his face. Again the stink of petrol filled the air. Crooke, nauseated with the smell and fear of what must be going to happen next, drew his revolver and fired a wild shot at the disappearing Storch. He missed by a mile.

'What the hell are they up to?' Stevens asked, clutching his bleeding face and staring after the plane which had swooped low over the palms preparatory for its next attack.

'The Count and the General are going to do a bunk!' he yelled above the roar of the Condor's engines.

'How?' the guardsman yelled. 'We've got 'em by the short hairs as long as we cover the strip!'

The Fieseler Storch was coming in again, low over the palms. The volume of the Egyptian fire increased, obviously trying to make them keep heads down during its overflight.

'Look at the grass!' Crooke pointed to the petrol-soaked yellow grass. 'They're going to set it alight! Make a smoke screen!' He dropped hastily, catching a glimpse of the man poised at the cabin door with the Verey pistol held in his hand. The Storch was a hundred yards away now. With trembling fingers he fired again and missed. Suddenly a tall figure pushed him to one side so that he nearly overbalanced in his awkward kneeling position. It was the American. He jumped on the boulder.

'Get down, you bloody fool!' he yelled.

The American did not hear. He stood there, swaying, the Schmeisser machine pistol cradled in his arms. Everywhere from among the trees the snipers concentrated their fire upon him. Bullets filled the air around him. The roar of the plane grew louder again.

'Fire, man! For God's sake, fire!' Crooke yelled.

But the American had only one mag left. He wasn't going to waste it. A bullet hit him. He staggered alarmingly, but didn't fall. Blood trickled down his bare leg. The Storch was almost above them. Its roar was ear-splitting. It seemed to be heading directly for the lone figure standing swaying on the rock. He was hit again, in the shoulder. Still he did not falter. At the cabin door a dark-faced man sat poised ready to set the petrol alight. Crooke could see every detail of his face. Suddenly the American sprang into action. A line of red holes zipped across the dark-faced man's chest. His mouth dropped open in a silent scream. He collapsed over the metal support, the pistol falling from his fingers.

The American fired again – one long, last burst.

The Condor was now edging its way on to the landing strip, cloaked in a huge cloud of dust. All four props whirling at full pitch, it began to bounce forward at an ever increasing rate.

Abruptly, as the American lowered his empty Schmeisser, the perspex of the Storch's cabin splintered. The pilot threw up his hands above his face in horror and self-protection. The next instant he disappeared from view behind the sudden spiderweb of smashed glass.

'You got the bastard!' Someone yelled. *'Yer did it, yer sodding Yank!'*

At two hundred miles an hour the blinded plane zoomed down in one last dive.

The Condor rolled forward. As yet its pilot had not seen the stricken Storch. The two planes rushed to meet each other.

'God Almighty!' Stevens breathed in awe.

Smoke, licked by evil little red flames, was pouring from the Storch's fuselage. It crept up around the man hanging from the open cockpit door. The Condor's tail wheel was coming up. Its flaps began to move. It was rolling along at 150 mph or more. A few seconds and the great four-engined plane would be airborne.

They stared at in awe, aware of the horror to come. Suddenly the Condor's pilot spotted the Storch diving straight for him. Instinctively he swung the Condor round. The port tyres burst like an 88 mm shell exploding. The great plane dipped. One wing struck the ground and snapped off. The Condor shimmied crazily. Desperately the pilot tried to right it and get out of the way of the flaming Storch diving straight at him But he was too late. There was a tremendous crash. At over two hundred miles an hour, the burning Storch struck the Condor broadside on. A huge wheel flew crazily through the air. The awe-struck watchers in the boulders ducked as it hurled over their heads, still turning. Fire broke out almost at once in the plane's rear. Green and red tracer ammo began zig-zagging crazily up into the sky. There was a series of muffled explosions.

It seemed a long time before the port door was finally flung open. A small wizened figure staggered out, his clothes ragged and smouldering. His legs wobbled as he dropped to the ground. For a moment he seemed bewildered. Then he raised his hands and began walking slowly towards them, blood pouring down his side, his thin voice crying: 'I surrender. I surrender.' Over and over again.

Among the palms, the rifle fire died away. A young officer rose, looked in disgust at El Nouri, who was only fifty yards from the British positions now, and snapped something in Arabic to the soldiers still hidden in the trees. He, too, raised his arms and started to walk towards them. Slowly, hesitantly, more and more soldiers emerged from their cover, dropping their weapons and following him into captivity. Behind them, the two wrecked planes, locked in crazy promiscuity were burning fiercely.

The little General, whom they had come so far to find, halted five yards away from the line of boulders and dropped his hands defiantly. The blood was pouring from a jagged wound in his side, but the hate in his eyes had not vanished.

'I surrender,' he said in thick guttural English, 'I surrender under duress.' He winced with pain and bit his bottom lip. The blood was staining the sand now. But he was a brave old man, brought up in the harsh tradition of the old pre-war Turkish *askaris*. 'But I still hate you...' he faltered and said weakly, 'but there will be another time.'

Crooke stared at him coldly. The man was a traitor to the Empire and deserved what he got, but he was a brave man all the same.

'Thaelmann,' he commanded, 'give me the bag please.'

Painfully Thaelmann reached down with his good hand and handed Crooke the bag which they had fashioned from an old piece of canvas taken from the old Bedford.

Crooke nodded and undid it. Carefully he brought out one of the sun-polished white objects, then the other. El Nouri Pasha forget his pain. His mouth, beneath the square, box-like moustache of the type affected by the old Turkish officers, dropped open in awe and bewilderment.

'What are those?' he said, reaching out a trembling hand to point at them.

'They are the skulls of Colonel Youngblood,' he lowered his voice and said gently, 'and your son, El Nouri Pasha.'

Slowly he turned them round so that the old man and the crowd of dark-faced, open-mouthed soldiers behind him could see the two neat bullet holes in the back of the heads.

'Youngblood and your son, both shot in the back of the skull. Murdered!'

The old man's skinny brown hand flew to

his throat. He clutched at it, as if he were being strangled.

'You mean, that man – that German...'

He broke off and pointed to the plane, his mouth forming the words, but no sound emerging from his trembling lips.

Crooke nodded.

'Eeh!' a strange eerie howl escaped from the old man's lips at last. He flung up both hands to the heavens in misery. 'My son – to die like that!'

There was a sudden crash over by the plane. Their gaze turned in its direction. The remaining wing had collapsed, dragging the burning fuselage over with it. A great section of the belly and side had peeled off under the impact. But that wasn't all.

A figure was stumbling from the crippled plane's body.

'Oh my God!' Stevens moaned.

Instead of a face, it had only a black crusted mask, where the eyes should have been there were two vivid scarlet pools. With agonizing slowness, the thing raised one charred hand, through which the bones gleamed whitely, and started to totter blindly towards them, trying to feel its way.

No one moved. Egyptian, German, British – they all stood petrified as the monstrous thing came closer and closer, the red hole of its mouth uttering strange inhuman sounds that could have signified anything.

Once it stumbled over one of the dead Brandenburgers. But it righted itself in time in a strangely stiff manner, that one obscene limb still stretched out in front of it.

A hundred yards – seventy – fifty. The Egyptians, their hands still raised, their dark faces a sickly hue, opened on both sides to let the apparition pass.

Then the thing stopped, as if it sensed they were there, waiting for it. It opened the hole that had once been a mouth. Meaningless sounds emerged as the charred body, the flesh hanging in dull red strips, swayed back and forth.

'Don't...' intelligible sounds came from the monster.

'Don't ... give ... up ... the credit ... of discovery...' The horrible burned claw searched for El Nouri's face.

He reeled back. 'You killed my son!' he cried.

The head of the thing turned stiffly in the direction of El Nouri's voice. The two suppurating scarlet pits stared into nothing.

Abruptly El Nouri acted. His eye had already fallen on the Verey pistol lying in the sand where the man in the plane had dropped it in the moment of his death.

'Get back,' he yelled at the defenders, and grabbed the brass-muzzled pistol. Crooke and the others tumbled back behind the cover of their rocks. The Egyptians scattered in haste. If he fired it in the petrol-laden atmosphere, there would be an immediate flash-fire. But El Nouri raised the pistol and quite deliberately took aim.

'Where ... are you?' the figure asked.

Somehow or other it sensed where the General was standing. Like a puppet gone wild, it started to totter towards its murderer. El Nouri screamed something in Arabic. There was a crack; a long stream of white shot from the pistol. It struck the thing squarely on the chest. It staggered as if it had blundered into an unseen gate. For a moment nothing happened. Then a ball of flame ignited its chest. It fell, wreathed in the ugly red light.

'Get down!' Crooke screamed at the top of his voice.

Not a moment too soon. An instant later, the desert directly in front of them exploded. One great, all-consuming flame reached up to the sky and vanished almost as soon as it had appeared, leaving behind it nothing but silence and the terrible, charred thing, crumpled up on the scorched sand. And all that was left to mark the thing's passing was a small round, fire-buckled plate of antique gold, the figure that had been etched in it so many centuries before with such loving care, gone – consumed in that all destroying fire.

Slowly the wind began to rise. As the survivors emerged from their state of paralysed horror, the sand started to drift in again from the desert, dusting its first light covering over the charred thing which had once been a man. It was all over. Soon Count Kun would be hidden by its soft brown blanket, joining those he had sought for so long in their centuries-old sleep.

6

Outside the bells from the little Gothic church across the flat November countryside were still pealing their joy. But the little group in dark-blue naval battledress congregated nervously in the great, timbered reception hall of Chequers, had no ears for the bells. Their attention was focused on the huge doors to the dining-room through which he would soon come. They could hear the noise and rattle of cutlery and the occasional burst of hearty VIP laughter, rich, unrestrained, full of its own importance.

Mallory looked at them. They looked smart and efficient in their dyed Navy battledress, their petty officer peaked caps clasped under their arms, most of their chests ablaze with medal ribbons, half of which they must have gained, he reasoned, in everything from the Abe Lincoln Battalion of the International Brigade to the 1st Battalion of the Foreign Legion. He wondered if it were against King's Regulations to wear them, but decided that it didn't really matter; he had already thrown the book out of the window by having them transferred bodily to the Royal Navy, without asking the Army first, and then equipping them with his self-designed unit patch – a white skull against a sea-blue background with the initials 'MD' – 'Mallory's Destroyers' – superimposed in blood red.

'My God, Miles,' Godfrey had snorted when he had first seen Sub-Lieutenant

Crooke, RNVR, wearing the patch, 'the Admiralty will have your guts for garters if they ever see that!'

'It adds that note of distinction, don't you think, Admiral?' But now he wondered what might happen if the top brass spotted it. 'Probably posted to Newcastle upon Tyne to inspect the construction of naval boilers,' he told himself in mock apprehension.

The bells continued to toll, like those of every church throughout the country, celebrating the victory at El Alamein. The group stared about them, their faces still showing the newly-healed scars of their wounds. Crooke, an ugly weal running down the left side of his face underneath the patch, wandered over to admire one of the great canvases on the wall. Gippo limped over to the huge antique table at which the great man himself worked, according to the man-servant who had ushered them in.

Dressed in officer's quality battledress, tailored for him on the Cairo black market as soon as they had heard they were being flown to the United Kingdom, he stared in feigned admiration at the odds and ends spread out over the table's gleaming oak surface. His black eyes flickered left and right. No one was watching him. Swiftly his fingers flashed out and seized the heavy silver-framed photograph of the wife of the man they had come so far to see.

He had already half-opened his battledress blouse when Crooke's voice said softly,

'Gippo!'

He looked up startled.

Crooke's one blue eye was staring back at him from the great gilded mirror over the open hearth.

'Put it back – *please*.'

A little shame-faced, he replaced it on the desk, fussing with it, as if he were only admiring the lady.'

'Sorry, sir,' he muttered.

Mallory shook his head and turned to Crooke.

'Well, your happy little band of brothers are certainly living up to their reputation,' he said. 'One day when all this disgusting business is over, I should like to write a novel about this lot, but no editor would ever believe such a bunch of villains could exist – even in fiction!'

The side door opened. Mallory turned round. But it wasn't the man they were waiting for. This man was small, lean and dressed in khaki, with the badges of rank of a field marshal. Mallory's heart sank. It was

'Brookie' – Field Marshal Alanbrooke, the bird-watching Ulsterman who was the Chief of the Imperial General Staff.

'So you're here, are you, Commander Mallory?' he snapped and deposited his battered brown brief-case on a chair, flashing them a hard searching look.

Mallory felt like replying that that was pretty damned obvious but confined himself to 'Yessir.'

Then Brooke's eagle eye had spotted the unit sign.

'You,' he ordered and crooked his finger at Peters. 'Come here.'

The guardsman did Mallory proud. He marched across the great room with his big chest stuck out, as if he were on parade in front of the King himself. With a tremendous noise that rang right up to the rafters, he stamped to attention in front of the Field Marshal and bellowed at the top of his voice: *'Sir!'* Brooke's face softened a little. For a moment he stared at the badge, then turned to Mallory, while the guardsman stared severely ahead into nothing.

'What exactly is this badge, Commander? What do the initials mean – MD?' he repeated the letters curiously. 'MD.'

Mallory raised an elegant finger to point at

the red initials, thinking hard. A whole range of interpretations raced through his mind. 'Mallory's Defectors... Mental Defectives...' 'Marine Detectors!' he snapped back smartly. 'They're a special branch of "Combined Ops", Field Marshal.'

'Hm,' Brooke absorbed the information. 'But why the death's head?'

Fortunately before Mallory had time to answer that question, the great doors at the end of the room opened and the brass started to come in – generals, admirals, with a sprinkling of ministers and high officials dressed in black jackets with striped trousers.

But it was not the military or the civilians who caught their eye; it was the pudgy cherubic man in a one-piece Bond-Street tailored 'siren suit', waving a cigar the size of a small pole in front of his wine-reddened face. He stamped by them, hardly giving them a glance and plumped himself down at the desk. For a moment the Prime Minister sat there in silence puffing his huge cigar, studying their faces while the brass arranged themselves respectfully behind him.

His eyes, running along the line, stopped at the purple ribbon of the VC on the one-eyed officer's chest. He looked up at

Crooke's hard face, visibly made a mental note, then queried in that well-remembered voice, akin at times to a snarl,

'Who are these men?'

'May I introduce them, Prime Minister?' Brooke said. 'They're the men who were involved in the El Nouri affair.' Swiftly he sketched the details in his precise general staff officer's manner, while Churchill, his eyes suddenly sullen for some reason known only to himself, sat there like the Chinese God of Plenty suffering from belly ache.

There was silence when he had finished. No one spoke – no one *dared* speak. Even the sheer incredibility of Mallory's men's long chase after El Nouri through unexplored desert could not move these men. The man who ruled the destiny of the British Empire and who was this day celebrating his first real victory in over two years of defeat, stared at them for what seemed a very long time.

'Ah yes,' he said at last, puffing out a wreath of expensive smoke and casting a glance at Mallory, 'you're the people whom the DNI calls "Mallory's Destroyers", aren't you?'

Out of the corner of his eye Mallory could see Brooke's hard jaw tighten, as if he had suddenly realized what the initials 'MD' meant. Thank God he had already been awarded his DSO for the action; Brooke would ensure there'd be no more gongs for him for the duration.

Churchill was obviously in high good humour. He turned to the severe-faced brass behind him and said:

'Last year I stated publicly that if Hitler invaded Hell itself, I would say a good word for the devil if necessary. Not' – he hesitated momentarily – 'that I would like it to leave this room that I compare our dear ally Josef Stalin with the devil, of course.' His eyes sparkled naughtily. 'Now it seems I have my own bunch of hired killers, eh!'

He chuckled at his own humour and pointed his huge cigar at the soldiers like a baton. 'It may interest you to know that our good and most loyal ally El Nouri Pasha has now been reinstated in his post due to the good offices of our minister in Cairo. His Majesty has also been gracious enough to award him the CBE for his great contribution to our noble victory in the Western Desert.'

His face creased in a huge grin. Behind him the brass tittered politely. Brooke continued to frown, as if he were making mental notes on the men lined up behind Mallory for use at some future date.

'It will keep Egypt quiet for a while. But only for a while. Their rapacious natures will soon want more.' His eyes suddenly lost their humour. Abruptly they were those of a man still faced with ordeal and great tragedy to come. 'But we shall attend to that when the time is ripe,' he concluded, as if to himself.

Then he was businesslike again. 'I am pleased, Commander Mallory, very pleased. You have done a good job of work.' For one long moment he looked at their faces: Gippo's eyes, dark and still searching for booty; Stevens, contained, cunning, Cockney; the American, lean, yellow and hard; Peters, staring rigidly at some far object like the good soldier he was; Thaelmann, curious yet somehow contemptuous at the visible signs of capitalistic power all around him; and Crooke, the one hard-blue eye burning with fanatical admiration for the man who had sworn that he had not become the King's First Minister to preside over the dissolution of the British Empire. Churchill took a pair of glasses from their case and, perching them on the end of his nose, peered down at the dossier in front of him. The interview was over.

Brooke gave one final bitter look, then nodded to Mallory. He gave a soft order. They swung round and began to move to the great doors. No one at the table seemed to notice. A servant opened the great doors, as if he had been listening at the keyhole outside, ready for this moment.

Suddenly Churchill raised his head from the midst of the brass bent down around him. That great voice which had brought shivers of delight and hope to millions of British people the world over in these last black years said:

'If you are murderers, as they say you are, let me have more of you. Mallory's Destroyers, we shall have need of you again – soon!'

And with that the doors closed behind them and they emerged into the damp English air, the bells of victory, heralding the start of the long road ahead, filling the grey sky.

The publishers hope that this book has given you enjoyable reading. Large Print Books are especially designed to be as easy to see and hold as possible. If you wish a complete list of our books please ask at your local library or write directly to:

Dales Large Print Books
Magna House, Long Preston,
Skipton, North Yorkshire.
BD23 4ND

This Large Print Book, for people
who cannot read normal print,
is published under the auspices of

THE ULVERSCROFT FOUNDATION

... we hope you have enjoyed this book.
Please think for a moment about those
who have worse eyesight than you ...
and are unable to even read or enjoy
Large Print without great difficulty.

You can help them by sending a
donation, large or small, to:

**The Ulverscroft Foundation,
1, The Green, Bradgate Road,
Anstey, Leicestershire, LE7 7FU,
England.**
or request a copy of our brochure for
more details.

The Foundation will use all donations
to assist those people who are visually
impaired and need special attention
with medical research, diagnosis
and treatment.

Thank you very much for your help.